The door opened an

with that gorgeous smile of hers that lifted his heart and made Finn want to reach forward and, quite naturally, kiss her.

Which, to the surprise of both of them, he did. As if he'd done it every time she opened the door to him—when in fact it hadn't happened before. And despite the widening of her eyes in surprise, she kissed him back. Ahh, so good.

So he moved closer and savored that her mouth melded soft and tentative against his. Luscious and sweet and…

He stepped right in, pulled the door shut behind him, locking the world away from them, because he needed her in his arms, hidden from prying eyes.

She didn't push him away; far from it—her hands crept up to his neck and encircled him as she leaned into his chest. The kiss deepened into a question from him, an answering need from her that made his heart pound again, and he tightened his arms even more around her. Their lips pressed, tongues tangled, hands gripped each other until his head swam with the scent and the taste of her. Time passed, but as in all things, slowly reality returned.

Dear Reader,

Welcome back to The Midwives of Lighthouse Bay. Lighthouse Bay is a small seaside town on the eastern coast of Australia, with pastel houses, crofts on the cliffs, a soaring lighthouse and a bevy of dedicated midwives who love their work.

A year on from Ellie and Sam's journey to happiness, we find Trina, or Catrina, as Finn calls her, our night-duty midwife, spotlighted in her own love story.

Two years ago, Catrina lost her darling husband, Ed, and has spent her nights since then catching babies to avoid waking to the cold, empty space beside her in bed. But her boss, Ellie, is expecting a baby, and Catrina is offered daytime in-charge, so it's time to face the world.

Finlay Foley is a single dad with his own heartbreak and loss, but at least he has his daughter, a one-year-old little ray of sunshine called Piper. I loved Finn as Catrina's hero, and Piper is an absolute doll who brings out the beautiful dad that Finn is.

I hope you enjoy Finn and Catrina's story as they tentatively hold hands and move into the golden light and sands of Lighthouse Bay and their future together.

I wish you a delightful holiday in your mind as you read *Healed by the Midwife's Kiss*.

With warmest regards,

xx Fi

HEALED BY THE MIDWIFE'S KISS

FIONA MCARTHUR

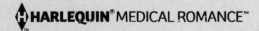

Recycling programs
for this product may
not exist in your area.

ISBN-13: 978-1-335-66342-9

Healed by the Midwife's Kiss

First North American Publication 2018

Copyright © 2018 by Fiona McArthur

All rights reserved. Except for use in any review, the reproduction or utilization of this work in whole or in part in any form by any electronic, mechanical or other means, now known or hereafter invented, including xerography, photocopying and recording, or in any information storage or retrieval system, is forbidden without the written permission of the publisher, Harlequin Enterprises Limited, 22 Adelaide St. West, 40th Floor, Toronto, Ontario M5H 4E3, Canada.

This is a work of fiction. Names, characters, places and incidents are either the product of the author's imagination or are used fictitiously, and any resemblance to actual persons, living or dead, business establishments, events or locales is entirely coincidental.

This edition published by arrangement with Harlequin Books S.A.

For questions and comments about the quality of this book, please contact us at CustomerService@Harlequin.com.

® and TM are trademarks of Harlequin Enterprises Limited or its corporate affiliates. Trademarks indicated with ® are registered in the United States Patent and Trademark Office, the Canadian Intellectual Property Office and in other countries.

Printed in U.S.A.

www.Harlequin.com

Dedicated to Finn, author Kelly Hunter's legend
of a four-legged friend who went to doggy heaven
while I was writing this book. It just seemed right
to say there are heroes named Finn everywhere.
Vale Finn.

**Praise for
Fiona McArthur**

"A book that was filled with plenty of emotion—
both happy and sad, two characters that need each
other to heal from their painful pasts and a story
line that illustrates love is worth fighting for."
—*Harlequin Junkie* on
A Month to Marry the Midwife

PROLOGUE

AT SIX A.M. on a Thursday, Lighthouse Bay's maternity ward held its breath. Midwife Catrina Thomas leaned forward and rubbed the newborn firmly with a warmed towel. The limp infant flexed and wriggled his purple limbs and finally took a gasping indignant lungful.

The baby curled his hands into fists as his now tense body suffused with pink. 'Yours now, Craig. Take him.' She gestured to the nervous dad beside her and mimed what to do as she encouraged Craig's big callused hands to gently lift the precious bundle. One huge splashing silver tear dropped to the sheet from his stubbled cheek as he placed his new son on his wife's warm bare stomach.

Craig released a strangled sob and his wife, leaning back on the bed in relief, half laughed in triumph, then closed her hands over her child and her husband's hands and pulled both upwards to lie between her breasts.

For Catrina, it was this moment. This snapshot in time she identified as her driver, the reason she felt she could be a midwife for ever—this and every other birth moment that had come before. It gave her piercing joy when she'd thought she'd lost all gladness, and it gave her bittersweet regret for the dreams she'd lost. But mostly, definitely, it gave her joy.

An hour later Catrina hugged her boss awkwardly, because Ellie's big pregnant belly bulged in the way as they came together, but no less enthusiastically because she would miss seeing her friend in the morning before she finished her shift. 'I can't believe it's your last day.' She rolled her eyes. 'Or my last night shift tomorrow.'

'Neither can I.' Ellie's brilliant smile lit the room even more than the sunlight streaming in through the maternity ward windows.

Trina marvelled at the pure happiness that radiated from a woman who had blossomed, and not just in belly size but in every way in just one year of marriage. Another reason

Trina needed to change her life and move on. She wanted what Ellie had.

A family and a life outside work. She would have the latter next week when she took on Ellie's job as Midwifery Unit Manager for Ellie's year of maternity leave.

She'd have daylight hours to see the world and evenings to think about going out for dinner with the not infrequent men who had asked her. The excuse of night shift would be taken out of her grasp. Which was a good thing. She'd hidden for two years and the time to be brave had arrived.

She stepped back from Ellie, picked up her bag and blew her a kiss. 'Happy last day. I'll see you at your lunch tomorrow.' Then she lifted her chin and stepped out of the door into the cool morning.

The tangy morning breeze promised a shower later, and pattering rain on the roof on a cool day made diving into bed in the daylight hours oh, so much more attractive than the usual sunny weather of Lighthouse Bay. Summer turning to autumn was her favourite time of year. Trina turned her face into the salty spray from the sea as she walked down towards the beach.

She slept better if she walked before going up the hill to her croft cottage, even if just a quick dash along the breakwall path that ran at right angles to the beach.

Especially after a birth. Her teeth clenched as she sucked in the salty air and tried not to dwell on the resting mother lying snug and content in the ward with her brand-new pink-faced baby.

Trina looked ahead to the curved crescent of the beach as she swung down the path from the hospital. The sapphire blue of the ocean stretching out to the horizon where the water met the sky, her favourite contemplation, and, closer, the rolling waves crashing and turning into fur-like foam edges that raced across the footprint-free sand to sink in and disappear.

Every day the small creek flowing into the ocean changed, the sandbars shifting and melding with the tides. The granite boulders like big seals set into the creek bed, lying lazily and oblivious to the shifting sand around them. Like life, Trina thought whimsically. You could fight against life until you realised that the past was gone and you needed to wait to see what the next tide brought. If only you could let go.

Ahead she saw that solitary dad. The one with his little girl in the backpack, striding along the beach with those long powerful strides as he covered the distance from headland to headland. Just like he had every morning she'd walked for the last four weeks. A tall, broad-shouldered, dark-haired man with a swift stride.

Sometimes the two were draped in raincoats, sometimes his daughter wore a cheery little hat with pom-poms. Sometimes, like today, they both wore beanies and a scarf.

Trina shivered. She could have done with a scarf. When she was tired it was easy to feel the cold. It would be good to move to day shifts after almost two bleak years on nights, but falling into bed exhausted in the daytime had been preferable to the dread of lying lonely and alone in the small dark hours.

She focused on the couple coming towards her. The little girl must have been around twelve months old, and seemed to be always gurgling with laughter, her crinkled eyes, waving fists and gap-toothed smile a delight to start the day with. The father, on the other hand, smiled with his mouth only when he barely lifted his hand but his storm-blue eyes glittered distant and broken beneath the dark brows. Trina didn't need to soak in anyone else's grief.

They all guessed about his story because, for once, nobody had gleaned any information and shared it with the inhabitants of Lighthouse Bay.

They drew closer and passed. 'Morning.' Trina inclined her head and waved at the little girl who, delightfully, waved back with a toothy chuckle.

'Morning,' the father said and lifted the corner of his lips before he passed.

And that was that for another day. Trina guessed she knew exactly how he felt. But she was changing.

CHAPTER ONE

Finn

AT SEVEN-THIRTY A.M. on the golden sands of Lighthouse Bay Beach Finlay Foley grimaced at the girl as she went past. Always in the purple scrubs so he knew she was one of the midwives from the hospital. A midwife. Last person he wanted to talk to.

It had been a midwife, one who put her face close to his and stared at him suspiciously, who told him his wife had left their baby and him behind, and ran away.

But the dark-haired girl with golden glints in her hair never invaded his space. She exuded a gentle warmth and empathy that had begun to brush over him lightly like a consistent warm beam of sunlight through leaves. Or like that soft shaft of light that reached into a corner of his cottage from the lighthouse on the cliff by some bizarre refraction. And always that feather-stroke of compassion without pity in her brown-eyed glance that thawed his frozen soul a little more each day when they passed.

She always smiled and so did he. But neither of them stopped. Thank goodness.

Piper gurgled behind his ear and he tilted his head to catch her words. 'Did you say something, Piper?'

'Mum, Mum, Mum, Mum.'

Finn felt the tightness crunch his sternum as if someone had grabbed his shirt and dug their nails into his chest. Guilt. Because he hadn't found her. He closed his eyes for a second. Nothing should be this hard. 'Try Dad, Dad, Dad, Dad,' he said past the tightness in his throat.

Obediently Piper chanted in her musical little voice, 'Dad, Dad, Dad, Dad.'

'Clever girl.' His mouth lifted this time and he felt a brief piercing of warmth from another beam of light in his cave-like existence.

Which was why he'd moved here. To make himself shift into the light. For Piper. And it did seem to be working. Something about this place, this haven of ocean and sand and cliffs and smiling people like the morning midwife soothed his ragged nerves and restored his faith in finding a way into the future.

A future he needed to create for Piper. Always the jolliest baby, now giggling toddler and all-round ray of puppy-like delight, Piper had kept him sane mainly because he had to greet each day to meet her needs.

His sister had said Piper had begun to look sad. Suspected she wasn't happy in the busy day care. Didn't see enough of her dad when he worked long hours. And he'd lifted his head and seen what his sister had seen.

Piper had been clingy. Harder to leave when he dropped her off at the busy centre. Drooping as he dressed her for 'school' in the morning. Quiet when he picked her up ten hours later.

Of course he needed to get a life and smile for his daughter. So he'd listened when his sister suggested he take a break from the paediatric practice where he'd continued as if on autopilot. Maybe escape to a place one of her friends had visited recently, where he knew no one, and heal for a week or two, or even a month for his daughter's sake. Maybe go back part-time for a while and spend more time with Piper. So he'd come. Here. To Lighthouse Bay.

Even on the first day it had felt right, just a glimmer of a breakthrough in the darkness, and he'd known it had been a good move.

The first morning in the guesthouse, when he'd walked the beach with Piper on his back, he'd felt a stirring of the peace he had found so elusive in his empty, echoing, accusing house. Saw the girl with the smile. Said, 'Good morning.'

After a few days he'd rented a cottage just above the beach for a week to avoid the other boisterous guests—happy families and young lovers he didn't need to talk to at breakfast—and moved to a place more private and offering solitude, but the inactivity of a rented house had been the exact opposite to what he needed.

Serendipitously, the cottage next door to that had come up for sale—*Would suit handyman*—which he'd never been. He was not even close to handy. Impulsively, after he'd discussed it with Piper, who had smiled and nodded and gurgled away his lack of handyman skills with great enthusiasm, he'd bought it. Then and there. The bonus of vacant possession meant an immediate move in even before the papers were signed.

He had a holiday house at the very least and a home if he never moved back to his old life. Radical stuff for a single parent, escaped paediatrician, failed husband, and one who had been used to the conveniences of a large town.

The first part of the one big room he'd clumsily beautified was Piper's corner and she didn't mind the smudges here and there and the chaos of spackle and paint tins and drip sheets and brushes.

Finally, he'd stood back with his daughter in his arms and considered he might survive the next week and maybe even the one after that. The first truly positive achievement he'd accomplished since Clancy left.

Clancy left.

How many times had he tried to grasp that fact? His wife of less than a year had walked away. Run, really. Left him, left her day-old daughter, and disappeared. With another man, if the private investigator had been correct. But still a missing person. Someone who in almost twelve months had never turned up in a hospital, or a morgue, or on her credit

card. He had even had the PI check if she
was working somewhere but that answer had
come back as a no. And his sister, who had
introduced them, couldn't find her either.

Because of the note she'd given the midwives, the police had only been mildly interested. Hence the PI.

*Look after Piper. She's yours. Don't try
to find me. I'm never coming back.*

That was what the note had said. The gossip had been less direct. He suspected what
the questions had been. Imagined what the
midwives had thought. *Why did his wife leave
him? What did he do to her? It must have
been bad if she left her baby behind...*

The ones who knew him well shook their
heads and said, *She'd liked her freedom too
much, that one.*

At first he'd been in deep shock. Then de-
nial. She'd come back. A moment's mad-
ness. She'd done it before. Left for days. With
the reality of a demanding newborn and his
worry making it hard for him to sleep at all,
his work had suffered. But his largest concern had been the spectre of Clancy with an

undiagnosed postnatal depression. Or, worse, the peril of a postnatal psychosis. What other reason could she have for leaving so suddenly so soon after the birth?

Hence he'd paid the private investigator, because there were no forensic leads—the police were inundated with more important affairs than flighty wives. But still no word. All he could do was pray she was safe, at least.

So life had gone on. One painful questioning new morning after another. Day after day with no relief. He hadn't been able to do his job as well as he should have and he'd needed a break from it all.

Buying the cottage had been a good move. Piper stood and cheered him on in her cot when he was doing something tricky, something that didn't need to have a lively little octopus climb all over him while he did it, and she waved her fists and gurgled and encouraged him as he learnt to be a painter. Or a carpenter. Or a tiler.

Or a cook. Or a cleaner. Or a dad.

He was doing okay.

He threw a last look out over the beach towards the grey sea and turned for home. 'That's our walk done for this morning, chicken. Let's go in and have breakfast. Then you can have a sleep and Daddy will grout those tiles in the shower so we can stop having bird baths in the sink.'

Piper loved the shower. Finn did too. When he held her soft, squirming satin baby skin against his chest, the water making her belly laugh as she ducked her head in and out of the stream always made him smile. Sometimes even made him laugh.

So he'd spent extra time on the shower. Adding tiles with animals, starfish, moon shapes and flowers, things they could talk about and keep it a happy place for Piper. And he'd made a square-tiled base with a plug. Soon she could have a little bath. One she could splash in even though it was only the size of the shower.

Doing things for Piper kept him sane. He didn't need the psychologist his sister said he did, or the medication his brother-in-law recommended. Just until he'd climbed out of the hole he'd dug himself to hide in, he would stay here. In Lighthouse Bay. Where nobody pointed or pitied him and every corner didn't hold a memory that scraped like fingernails on the chalkboard of his heavy heart.

Except that around the next corner his heart froze for a millisecond to see the morning midwife crouched on the path in front of him.

He quickened his pace. 'Are you okay?'

She turned to look up at him, cradling something brightly coloured against her chest, and with the shift of her shoulders he saw the bird cupped in her hands. 'She flew into that window and knocked herself out.'

The lorikeet, blue-headed with a red and yellow chest, lay limp with lime-green wings folded back in her hands. A most flaccid bird.

Still, the red beak and chest shuddered gently so it wasn't dead. 'How do you know it's a girl?' He couldn't believe he'd just said that. But he'd actually thought it was her that had been hurt and relief had made him stupid.

She must have thought he was stupid too. 'I didn't actually lift her legs and look. Not really of major importance, is it?'

Just a little bit of impatience and, surprisingly, it was good to be at the receiving end of a bit of healthy sarcasm. So much better than unending sympathy.

He held up his hands in surrender and Piper's voice floated over both of them from his back. 'Dad, Dad, Dad!'

The girl sucked in her breath and he could see her swan-like neck was tinged with pink. 'Sorry. Night duty ill temper.'

'My bad. All mine. Stupid thing to say. Can you stand up? It's tricky to crouch down with Piper on my back. Let's have a look at her.'

The morning midwife rose fluidly, calves of steel obviously; even he was impressed with her grace—must be all those uphill walks she did. 'She's not fluttering her wings,' she said, empathy lacing a voice that, had it not been agitated, would have soothed the bird. He shook himself. She was just being a typical midwife. That was how most of them had spoken to him when Clancy had disappeared.

'Still breathing.' He stroked the soft feathers as the bird lay in her small hands. 'She's limp, but I think if you put her in a box for a couple of hours in the dark, she'll rouse when she's had a sleep to get over the shock.'

'Do you think so?'

'I do. She's not bleeding. Just cover the box with a light cloth so she can let you know she can fly away when she's ready.'

'Do I have to put food or water in there?'

'Not food. A little water as long as she

doesn't fall into it and drown.' He grimaced at another stupid comment.

She grinned at him and suddenly the day was much brighter than it had been. 'Are you a vet?'

'No.'

'Just a bird wrangler?'

She was a stunner. He stepped back. 'One of my many talents. I'll leave you to it.'

'Thank you.'

'Bye.'

She looked at him oddly. Not surprising. He was odd. He walked on up the hill.

Her voice followed him. 'Bye, Piper.' He heard Piper chuckle.

CHAPTER TWO

Trina

TRINA FINISHED HER night shift at seven a.m. on Friday and picked up her mini-tote to sling it on her shoulder. Her last night done, except for emergencies, and she did a little skip as she came out of the door. At first, she'd been reluctant to take the night shift to day shift change that Ellie had offered her because change could be scary, but it had started the whole paradigm inversion that her life had needed. Look out daylight. Here she comes.

Yes. She'd come a long way in almost two years since Ed had died.

Not just because on Monday morning she'd return as acting Midwifery Unit Manager, an unexpected positive career move for Trina at Lighthouse Bay Maternity.

But things had changed.

Her grief stayed internal, or only rarely escaped under her pillow when she was alone in her croft on the cliff.

And since Ellie's wedding last year she'd begun to think that maybe, some time in the future, she too could look at being friends with a man. If the right one came along.

Not a relationship yet. That idea had been so terrifying, almost like PTSD——the fear of imagining what if history repeated itself; what if that immense pain of loss and grief hit her again? What then?

She'd been catatonic with that thought and to divert herself she'd begun to think of all the other things that terrified her. She'd decided to strengthen her Be Brave muscle.

Last week she'd had her first scuba lesson. Something that had fascinated but petrified her since she'd watched the movie *Finding Nemo* with the daughter of a friend. And in the sparkling cove around the corner from Lighthouse Bay the kindly instructor had been so reassuring, so patient, well… Maybe she'd go back on Saturday for another lesson.

And when she'd mastered that she was going out on a day of deep-sea fishing. The captain's wife had not long delivered a late-in-life baby and Trina had been the midwife. Even though he'd fainted again, he'd promised her a day of deep-sea fishing when he felt better. She'd bought seasickness bands and stored them in her drawer just in case.

She wasn't sure about the parachuting. The girls at work had all joined the idea factory and brochures and social media tags of extreme sports and adventure holidays appeared like magic in her pigeonhole and on her private page. Parachuting? She didn't think so but she'd worry about that later.

Her aim to do one challenge a month seemed possible to allay the fear that she was relying on work to be her whole world. Though not too adventurous—she didn't want to kill herself. Not now.

Her friends were cheering. Thinking of the midwives of Lighthouse Bay…well, that made her whole world warm into a rosy glow. A fiercely loyal flotsam of women tossed here by the fickle cruelty of life, forging into a circle of hands supporting birthing women and each other. All acutely aware of how fortunate they were to have found the magic of the bay.

There was something healing about that crescent of sand that led to the cliffs.

A mystical benevolence about the soaring white lighthouse on the tallest point that looked benignly over the tiny hamlet of coloured houses and shone reassuring light.

And the pretty pastel abodes like a quaint European seaside town were a delight, a new trend that had taken off with the gentle crayon façades dipping in colour like playful toes into the sea.

Crazy coloured houses, and if she could do all those crazy-coloured feats of bravery then just maybe she could be brave enough to begin a real conversation with a man. Like yesterday. She'd almost forgotten the handsome dad was a man when she'd snapped at him. They'd almost had a whole conversation. She wouldn't mind another one so he didn't think she was a short-tempered shrew but she had been concerned about the bird. The one that had flown away two hours later, just like he said it would.

If she could talk to a man she could try again to go out with one. At least once. She'd been turning them down for six months now. None of them had been Ed.

Now there were more midwives around to lessen the on-call restrictions. Four new midwives had come on board to swell their ranks with the shift to a midwife-led unit. They still had old Dr Southwell in the hospital for non-maternity patients and maternity emergencies, but all the midwives had moved to four days of ten-hour shifts and caring for a caseload of women, so suddenly there was more time for life with an extra day free and people to cover you if needed. And she'd scored the admin side Monday to Thursday, daylight hours, for a year. Starting Monday. Imagine.

So she'd better get out there and grab that exciting life before it drifted past in a haze of regrets. She lifted her head and sucked in a pure lungful of gorgeous sea air.

Without realising it her feet had followed the well-beaten path down to the beach and just as she turned to start her morning break-wall walk she saw the dad and his little girl come up off the beach.

He looked happier today. Nice. It made her smile warmer. 'Beautiful morning.'

He looked startled for a minute. 'Yes, it is.' Almost as if he was surprised. 'Good morning—how is your bird?'

'Flew away two hours later. Didn't look any worse for wear.'

He gave her the first real smile she'd seen. 'That's good.'

Then he was past. Trina turned her head to glance back and the little fair-haired girl waved.

Trina smiled and yawned. She should go to bed and get a couple of hours' sleep before Ellie's farewell lunch. Just a quick walk.

CHAPTER THREE

Finn

THE EARLY-MORNING BREEZE off the ocean seemed cooler. The water had taken till now to shine like a jewel. She'd been late this morning. Finn had waited a minute, hoping she wouldn't see him do it, and strangely the minute seemed to take for ever, then he'd looked back. He'd been thinking of her last night. Wondering if she were sad about a dead bird or happy when it flew away.

He thought back to her response. Now that was a smile. He could see it in his retina like a glance at the sun. Warm and glowing. Saw her walking quite a way in the distance— she'd moved fast. He'd noticed that before, that her pace ran to brisk rather than daw-dling. Nurses often did walk briskly. Couldn't seem to slow themselves enough to meander even on a seaside walk. He tore his eyes away.

He'd done the breakwall walk she did a couple of times when he'd first come here but he liked the effort of walking through the sand with Piper on his back. If nothing else he'd become fit and tanned and physically healthier here in a month. And Piper too had sun-kissed limbs and sparkling eyes that exuded health.

His sister would be pleased when she came today. His first visitor. He shied away from that intrusion into his safe world and thought again of the young midwife. Maybe not so young because he'd seen the signs of loss and life in her big coffee eyes—even in those brief glances they'd shot at each other. For the first time he wondered if other people had suffered as much as he had? Well, that at least seemed a positive sign that he could reconnect with his inherent compassion that he'd seemed to have lost.

The thought made him wonder what it would be like to talk to someone who could actually begin to understand his hell, and then called himself crazy for making up a past about someone he didn't know. Poor woman probably had never had a sad day in her life. But something told him otherwise.

Just before one p.m. his sister stepped out of her red convertible and through his front gate. 'It's beautiful, Finn. I can't believe you've done all this yourself!' Her perfectly pencilled brows were raised as she gazed at the pale pink external walls of the house and the rose-red door.

He'd been a little surprised himself. And the front path bordered by pansies and baby's breath looked as if it belonged to some older lady with a green thumb—not a guilt-deranged paediatrician running from life.

She rocked her head slowly. He'd expected disbelief but not this patent incredulity. He felt strangely offended. 'I didn't even know you like to garden!'

He shrugged, urging her towards the door. 'Neither did I. But Piper loves being outside and we needed to do something while we're out here.'

Frances rubbernecked her way up the path, nice and slow for the neighbours, he thought dryly, and sighed while she gushed. She gushed when she didn't know what to say, though what the problem was he had no idea.

'And the house. Freshly painted? You actually painted?' She glanced around. 'Pastel like the others in the street. It's gorgeous.'

Finn looked at the stucco walls. They'd been a pain to paint. 'Piper chose the colour. I would have preferred a blue but, given the choice, she went for pink every time. Never thought I'd have a stereotypical daughter.'

Frances laughed and waved her hand dismissively. 'Piper's too young to choose.'

'No, she's not,' he said mildly. 'How can you say it's not her choice if I give her four colours and she keeps choosing pink?'

Frances looked at him as if he needed a big dose of sympathy for his feeble brain. 'You didn't pretend she was choosing?'

'Who else was I going to ask?' He heard the edge in his voice. And his sister shut up. So then he felt mean.

It was always like this. On and on until he shut her down. She meant well, but for heaven's sake. He wanted her gone already.

They finally made it to the front door.

In an attempt to lighten the mood he stopped to show her something else. 'Piper helped everywhere.' He kissed the top of his daughter's head as she perched on his hip. Quiet for a change because she hadn't quite found her ease with her aunt. Or maybe she was picking up Finn's nervous vibes. Either way she leaned into him, unusually subdued.

He pointed to a handprint on the front step that he'd finished with instant cement. Using a layer of cling wrap over the wet surface, he'd pressed her starfish hand into the step on each side while holding her clamped to his side. The little palm prints made him smile every time he opened the door.

'Come in.' He heard the pride in his voice and mocked himself. Finn the decorator. 'There's still the kitchen and laundry, but I've finished Piper's corner, the bathroom and the floating boards on the floor because she'll need a solid surface to learn to walk on.'

Frances rotated her neck, as if stuck to the step and that was the only part of her body she could move. 'It's tiny.'

He frowned. 'Yes. It's a beach cottage. Not a mansion.'

She blinked. Shifted uneasily. 'Oh, yes. Of course. But your other beautiful house...'

'Is on the market.'

Now the shock was real. Frances had approved mightily of his imposing residence on top of the hill. Two hills over from her imposing residence. He'd only liked it because Clancy, his missing wife, had loved it.

Frances spluttered, 'You're buying a new house?'

'I've bought a new house.' He put out one hand and gestured. 'This house. I'm staying here.'

'I... I thought you'd done this for the owners. That you rented?'

'I am the owner.' *A little too fierce, Finn,* he chided himself.

Frances leaned towards him pleadingly. 'But your work?'

'Will be here too when I'm ready. One of the GPs here has offered me a place in his practice when I'm ready. I'll specialise in children but do all the GP stuff I've almost forgotten. It'll be good.' He wasn't sure who he was convincing, Frances or himself. 'It won't be yet because I'm in no hurry.'

'But...'

'But what?'

His sister turned worried eyes on his. 'You

were only supposed to come here for a few weeks and then come back. Come home.'

'Home to where, Frances? To what? To an empty castle on a hill full of ghosts and pain. To a clinic with not enough hours in the day so I had to keep my daughter in long day care?'

Frances looked stricken and he leaned in and shared a hug with her, Piper still a limpet on his other hip. Frances meant well and she truly loved him. And now that Mum was gone she was all the family he had. Of course she'd never understood him with the ten-year age difference. Frances hadn't understood Mum either, if they were being honest. 'It's okay. This is a magic place to live and for Piper and me this is the right place at the right time. We're staying.'

Frances almost wrung her hands. 'You won't meet any eligible women here.'

He could feel his mood slip further. His irritation rise. His disappointment deepen. His sister didn't understand his guilt couldn't be fixed by an eligible woman. 'Eligible for what, Frances? I'm no good for any woman at the moment and won't be…' he didn't say *ever* '…for a very long time.'

He decided not to demonstrate the shower. Or point anything else out. Ditched the plans to take a picnic to the beach.

Instead he took Frances to the most expensive restaurant in town, where Piper slept in her stroller beside the table despite the noise of conversations and laughter all around, and listened to her stories of droll people and dire events in her husband's practice.

In the corner of the restaurant he noticed a very attractive brunette. She nodded at him and he realised it was his morning midwife, elegantly dressed—*sans* scrubs—and made-up like a model, her brown hair blow-dried and shining, the glints catching the sun. Looking like a million bucks. Other men were looking at her. He preferred the wind-blown version.

She sat, a little isolated, in a lively group of people, all chinking champagne flutes to celebrate. Frances would approve of the clientele, he thought dryly, but recognised the older doctor he'd mentioned to his sister, and noted the stylish older woman next to him who leant into his shoulder, probably his wife. Another young woman he hadn't seen around was chatting to the vibrantly glowing woman in the latter stages of pregnancy who drank water, and next to her a man hovered protectively, obviously the doting father-to-be.

He wished him better luck than he'd had. Finn felt his heart twist in self-disgust. He'd tried that. A lot of good that had done him.

'Finn?'

His sister's voice called him back to the present and he jerked his face away from them. 'Sorry. You were telling me about Gerry's partner?'

Frances hovered over being cross for a moment and thankfully decided to forgive graciously. 'I was saying she has no idea how a doctor's wife should dress.'

The lunch dragged on until finally Piper woke up and gave him an excuse to pay the bill.

They waved Frances goodbye after lunch with much relief. 'Seriously, Piper. Your aunt is getting worse. We're lucky to be so far away.'

They took the sand buckets and spade back down to the beach in the afternoon because Piper's routine had been disrupted and she needed to get some play time in and wear herself out before bedtime.

To his surprise, and with a seagull-like swoop of uplifting spirits, the morning midwife sat there on the breakwall, back in beach clothes and mussed by the wind. He smiled at her like a long-lost friend. After the visit from his sister he felt as if he needed a pal.

CHAPTER FOUR

Trina

TRINA SAT SWINGING her legs on the breakwall down on the beach and breathed in the salt. The sea air blew strands into her eyes but it felt too good to worry about that. She saw him before he saw her and a deep, slashing frown marred his forehead. Different to this morning. Then his expression changed as he saw her, the etched lines disappeared and an unexpected, ridiculously sexy, warmly welcoming smile curved in a big sweep. *Goodness.* What had she done to deserve that?

'Lovely afternoon,' he said and the little girl waved.

Trina's mouth twitched as she waved back. 'Beautiful. I saw you at lunch. That's three times in a day.'

'A new world record,' he agreed and she blushed. No idea why.

He paused beside her, another world record, and looked down from far too high. Up close and stationary, told herself again, he would be a very good-looking man—to other women. She studied him almost dispassionately. Long lashes framed those brilliant blue eyes and his dark brown wavy hair curled a tad too long over his ears. His chin was set firm and his cheekbones bordered on harsh in the bright light. She could see his effort to be social cost him. She knew the feeling.

'I'm Catrina Thomas.' She didn't enlarge. He could ask if he was interested, but something told her he wasn't so much interested as in need of a friend. Which suited her perfectly.

'Finlay Foley. And you've met Piper. My daughter.' The little girl bounced in the backpack.

You could do nothing but smile at Piper. 'Piper looks like she wants to get down amongst the sand.'

'Piper is happiest when she's caked in sand.' His hand lifted to stroke the wiggling little leg at his chest. Strong brown fingers tickling a plump golden baby ankle. 'We're going to build sandcastles. Piper is going to play hard and long and get extremely tired so she will sleep all night.' Trina wasn't sure if he was telling her or telling Piper. She suspected the latter.

'Nice theory,' Trina agreed judiciously. 'I see you have it all worked out.'

He began to fiddle with the straps as he extricated his daughter from the backpack and clinically she watched the muscle play as man power pulled his loose white shirt tight. His thick dark hair tousled in the wind and drew her eyes until she was distracted again by the wriggling child. Finlay popped her down in the sand on her bottom and put a spade and bucket beside her.

'There, miss.' He glanced up at Trina. 'Her aunt came today and she's ruined our sleep routine.' He paused at that. 'Speaking of routines, this is late in the day for you to be on the beach.'

'Nice of you to notice.' She wasn't sure if it was. There had been a suspicious lift of her spirits when she'd realised the woman he'd shared lunch with was his sister. What was that? She didn't have expectations and he wouldn't either—not that she supposed he would have. She wasn't ready for that. 'Don't get ideas or I'll have to leave.' Almost a joke. But she explained.

'Today is my first official Friday off for a long time. I'm off nights and on day shifts for the next year. Monday to Thursday.' She looked around at the little groups and families on the beach and under the trees at the park. Pulled a mock frowning face. 'I'll have to talk to people and socialise, I guess.'

'I know. Sucks, doesn't it.' The underlying truth made them both stop and consider. And smile a little sheepishly at each other.

Another urge to be truthful came out of nowhere. 'I'm a widow and not that keen on pretending to be a social butterfly. Hence the last two years on night duty.'

He said more slowly, as if he wasn't sure why he was following suit either, 'My wife left us when Piper was born. A day later. I've morphed into antisocial and now I'm hiding here.'

Died? Or left? How could his wife leave when their daughter was born? She closed her mouth with a snap. Not normal. Something told her Piper's mum hadn't died, though she

didn't know why. Postnatal depression then?
A chilling thought. Not domestic violence?

As if he read her thoughts, he added, 'I
think she left with another man.' He seemed
to take a perverse pleasure in her disbelief.
'I need to start thinking about going back to
work soon. Learn to stop trying to guess what
happened. To have adult conversations.'

He shrugged those impressive shoulders.
Glanced around at the white sand and waves.
'I'm talking to Piper's dolls now.'

Still bemused by the first statement, the
second took a second to sink in. Surprisingly,
Trina giggled. She couldn't remember the last
time she'd giggled like a schoolgirl.

He smiled and then sobered. 'Which means
Piper and her dolls must go into day care if I
go back to work.'

'That's hard,' Trina agreed but wondered
what sort of work he could 'start thinking
about going back to'. Not that there were
screeds of choices around here. 'Maybe part-
time?'

'I think so.'

'Are you a builder? The house looks good.'

He laughed at that. 'No. Far from it. Piper's
taught me everything I know.'

Trina giggled again. *Stop it.* She sounded like a twit. But he was funny. 'I didn't have you pegged as a comedian.'

His half-laugh held a hint of derision at himself. 'Not usually. Remember? Antisocial.'

She nodded with solemn agreement. 'You're safe with me. If you need a protected space to tell your latest doll story you can find me.' She waited until his eyes met hers. 'But that's all.'

'Handy to know. Where do I find you? You know where I live.' Then he turned away as if he regretted asking.

'Of course I know where you live. It's a small town and single men with babies are rare.' Trina looked at him. 'I meant…find me here. But I'll think about it. I'm happy to have a male friend but not a stalker.'

She felt like an idiot saying that but thankfully he just looked relieved. 'Hallelujah. And I promise I will never, ever turn up uninvited.'

'We have that sorted.' She glanced at Piper, who sat on the sand licking white granules off her fingers, and bit back a grin. 'It's good when children will eat anything.'

Finn focused instantly on his daughter and

scooped her up. Trina could see him mentally chastising himself. She imagined something like, *See what happens when you don't concentrate on your daughter*, and she knew he'd forgotten her. Was happy for the breathing space because, speaking of breathing, she was having a little trouble.

She heard his voice from a long way away. 'Sand is for playing—not eating, missy.' He scooped the grains from her mouth and brushed her lips. His quick glance brushed over Trina as well as he began to move away. 'Better go wash her mouth out and concentrate. Nice to meet you, Catrina.'

'You too,' she said, suddenly needing to bolt home and shut her door.

Ten minutes later the lock clunked home solidly and she leant back against the wood. Another scary challenge achieved.

Not that she'd been in danger—just a little more challenged than she'd been ready for. And she had been remarkably loose with her tongue. Told him she was a widow. About her job. The hours she worked. What had got into her? That was a worry. So much so that it did feel incredibly comforting to be home. Though, now that she looked around, it seemed dark inside. She frowned. Didn't just *seem* dark.

Her home was dark.

And just a little dismal. She frowned and then hurried to reassure herself. Not tragically so, more efficiently gloomy for a person who slept through a lot of the daylight hours. She pulled the cord on the kitchen blind and it rolled up obediently and light flooded in from the front, where the little dead-end road finished next door.

She moved to the side windows and thinned the bunching of the white curtains so she could see through them. Maybe she could open those curtains too. Now that she'd be awake in the daytime. Moving out of the dark, physically and figuratively.

So, she'd better see to lightening it up. Maybe a few bright cushions on her grey lounge suite; even a bright rug on the floor would be nice. She stared down at the grey and black swirled rug she'd bought in a monotone furnishing package when she moved in. Decided she didn't like the lack of colour.

She crossed the room and threw open the heavy curtains that blocked the view. Unlocking the double glass doors and pushing them slowly open, she stepped out onto her patio to look out over the glittering expanse of ocean that lay before her like a big blue shot-thread quilt as far as the eye could see. She didn't look down to the beach, though she wanted too. Better not see if there was the figure of a man and a little girl playing in the waves.

Instead she glanced at the little croft to her right where Ellie and Sam lived while Sam built the big house on the headland for their growing family. She wondered if they would keep the croft, as they said they would. It would be strange to have new neighbours on top of everything else.

The three crofts sat like seabirds perched on a branch of the headland, the thick walls painted white like the lighthouse across the bay and from the same solid stone blocks. Trina's veranda had a little awning over the deck the others lacked. A thick green evergreen hedge separated the buildings to shoulder height.

On the other side of her house lay Myra's croft. Originally from Paddington in Sydney, stylish Myra ran the coffee shop at the hospital and had recently married the older Dr Southwell—her boss Ellie's father-in-law.

Two brides in two months, living each side of her, and maybe that had jolted her out of her apathy as much as anything else. Surrounded by people jumping bravely into new relationships and new lives had to make a woman think.

She stepped out and crossed to the two-person swing seat she'd tussled with for hours to assemble. Her last purchase as a flat-pack. Last *ever*, she promised herself.

She'd never seen so many screws and bolts and instructions in one flat-pack. Then she'd been left with a contraption that had to be dragged inside when it got too windy here on top of the cliffs because it banged and rattled and made her nervous that it would fly into the ocean on a gust. It wasn't really that she thought about the fact it needed a second person. Not at all.

She stepped back inside, glanced around then picked up the sewing basket and dug in it for the ribbons she'd put away. Went back to the double doors and tied back the curtains so they were right off the windows. Not that she was getting visitors—her mind shied away from the mental picture of a man and his baby daughter.

No. She'd lighten it because now she didn't need to exclude the light to help her sleep. She was a day-shift person. She was brave. And tomorrow she'd scuba again, and maybe talk to Finlay and Piper if she saw them because she was resurrecting her social skills and stepping forward. Carefully.

CHAPTER FIVE

Finn

FINN GLANCED BACK to the rocky break-wall once, to the spot where Catrina—nice name—had disappeared, as he crouched with Piper at the edge of the water to rinse her mouth of sand. It seemed other people did hurt like he did. And were left with scars that impacted hugely on how they lived their lives.

Two years working on night duty. He shuddered but could see the logic. Side-stepping the cold space beside you in the bed at night and avoiding that feeling of loss being the first thing you noticed in the day. Maybe he should have given that a go.

But the way she'd said she hadn't pegged him as a comedian surprised him out of his usual lethargy. He'd made her laugh twice— that was pretty stellar. Apart from his daughter, whose sense of humour ran to very simple slapstick, he hadn't made anyone giggle for a long time. He could almost hear her again. Such a delicious giggle. More of a gurgle really.

So—a widow? Lost like him, for a different reason. He wondered how her husband had died but in the end it didn't really change her pain. He was gone. For ever. Unlike the uncertainty he lived with.

Would Clancy ever come back? In a year. In ten years? Was she even alive? But, most of all, what would he tell Piper when she grew up? How could he say her mother loved her when she'd walked away and never asked about her again? The pain for Piper's future angst had grown larger than his own loss and he had no desire to rush the explanations.

Milestones with Piper never passed without him singeing himself with bitterness that Clancy wasn't there to see them. First tooth. First word. First step last week—though she still spent most of her time on her bottom. And on Sunday—first birthday. He felt his jaw stiffen. That would be the day he said *enough*. Enough holding his breath, expecting Clancy to walk through the door.

A milestone he'd never thought he'd get to. He hadn't decided whether to stay in Lighthouse Bay for the day with their usual routine; he was leaning towards taking Piper shopping, something he loathed, so that the logistics of strollers and car parking and crowd managing with a toddler drowned out the reminders of the best day of his life twelve months ago that had changed so soon after.

He wondered suddenly if he could ask Catrina to come. As a diversion, a pseudo-mother for the day, and then found himself swamped by such intense anger at Clancy for leaving their daughter he almost moaned. Piper clutched his hand and he looked down to see his daughter's eyes staring up at him as if she could sense his pain.

He scooped her up and hugged her, felt the lump in his chest and willed it away. Whatever they did, he needed to remember it was a celebration of this angel in his arms, not of the woman who'd left them.

'I'll always love you, darling.' The words came out thickly. 'What would you like to do on Sunday, Piper?'

'Mum, Mum, Mum, Mum.'

He groaned and buried his face in her

shimmering golden cloud of hair. Fine mist-like hair that floated in the breeze and tangled if he didn't tie it back but he couldn't bring himself to get it cut. His gorgeous little buttercup with her fine-spun headache of hair.

'Mum, Mum, Mum,' Piper chirped.

The last thing he needed to hear at this moment. 'Oh, baby, don't. Please.'

She squirmed and the baby voice drifted up to him. Uncertain. 'Dad, Dad, Dad, Dad?'

Pull yourself together. He lifted his head and looked into the soft dimpled face so close to his. 'Yes. Dad, Dad, Dad, Dad.' He carried her into the waves to dangle her feet and she wriggled happily. He concentrated on his fingers holding her as he swept her ankles through the waves and the foam ran up her knees as she squealed in delight. Guilt swamped him all over again. 'You can say *Mum, Mum, Mum* any time, my darling. Of course you can. Daddy's being silly.' *Stupid!*

Piper gurgled with laughter. 'Dad, Dad, Dad, Dad.' Finn could feel his heart shattering into a million pieces again and any lingering thoughts of Catrina the midwife washed into the sea with the grains of sand stuck to Piper's feet.

CHAPTER SIX

Trina

THE EARLY-MORNING SUNBEAM poked Trina in the eye with an unfamiliar exuberance and she groaned and threw her hand up to cover her face. *Who left the curtains open?* Only one answer to that. The twinge of morning memory and loss made her breath hitch and she forced herself to breathe calmly.

Saturday morning. Scuba lesson. She groaned again and all the doubts and fears from last week came rushing back to twist her stomach. Why had she said she wanted to do this again? Why the need to push herself to extremes she didn't feel comfortable with?

She flung the bedclothes back and swung her legs. The floor was warmed a little under her feet from the sun. That too seemed different.

Okay. Why was she fighting this? This was a new chapter in her life. Same book. She wasn't removing any of the pages—just going forward.

She squinted at the morning beams painting the inside of her one-room croft in golden stripes and decided they were quite lovely. Not worth groaning about at all.

She padded across to the uncurtained double doors looking out over the ocean and decided the light streaming in shone still a little too bright until she'd made an Earl Grey to start the day and turned her back.

As she busied herself in the tiny kitchen nook, she pondered on yesterday and the advances she'd made towards holding a sensible conversation with an eligible male. Though technically she guessed he wasn't eligible. But probably safe to practise on, as long as he was okay with it.

Not that she had any long-term intentions but she'd done all right. Beaten the bogeyman, and so had he. That made it a little easier. And no doubt different for him, as his wife had chosen to go. How on earth could a woman leave her baby? And why would she leave Finlay? That too was a teensy worry.

Trina thought back to where she'd been a year ago. Still in a black fog with a bright shiny mask on her face for work.

She didn't believe that time healed all wounds, but maybe it scabbed over some of the deeper lacerations. The problem with losing your true love was they were never really gone, always hovering, a comfort, and an ache that flared into pain that burned right through you.

Boy, did she recognise the symptoms of reluctantly dipping a toe into the real world after the misty haze of deep grief. There were some aspects of her loss of Ed that would never disappear but in other ways she could, and would, live a happy life. She didn't think that Finlay Foley had reached that stage yet. Which was a tiny shame.

But she'd better get on and prepare for her scuba lesson. She'd eat when she came back.

By the time Trina left her croft on the cliff she knew she'd be late if she didn't hurry and her steps skipped as she descended to the beach with her towel and specially fitted snorkelling mask. That was one good thing about living right on the beach—she didn't need to carry much because home was always a few steps away.

The path stopped at the sand and Trina began walking quickly around the headland. She'd glanced once towards the curve of the bay but no Finlay and Piper there, no sign of him, so tall and broad and unmistakable, so no golden-haired Piper on his back either, and fancifully it felt strange to be hurrying away without seeing them.

She forced herself to look forward again and concentrated on the scuba lessons she'd learnt last week from old Tom, running through the procedures.

'Nice even breathing through the mouth-piece; no holding your breath. This is how to replace a regulator in your mouth if it gets knocked out. This is how to control the speed of your ascent and descent by letting air in and out via the buoyancy control, so your ears don't hurt. Nothing to be nervous about. We'll go as slow as you need.'

Two hours later as she walked home in a much more desultory fashion a glow of pride warmed her as she remembered old Tom's quiet pleasure in her. 'You're a natural,' he'd told her.

A natural scuba diver? Who would have known? But today he'd taken her to the little island just off the beach and they'd dived slowly around the tiny inlets and rocks and seen colourful fish, delicate submarine plant life that swayed with the rhythm of the ocean, once a small stingray and one slightly larger shark, and it had all been Technicolor brilliant. Exciting. And, to her absolute delight, she'd loved it.

Her mind danced with snapshots of the morning and she didn't see the man and little girl sitting in a shallow rock pool under the cliff until she was almost upon them.

'Oh. You. Hello,' she stammered as she was jerked out of her happy reveries.

'Good morning, Catrina,' Finlay said. Though how on earth he could remain nonchalant while sitting in a sandy-bottom indent in the rock where the water barely covered his outstretched legs, she had no idea. 'You look very pleased with yourself.'

She regarded them. She liked the way they looked—so calm and happy, Piper dressed in her frilly pink swimsuit that covered her arms and legs. And she liked the way he called her Catrina. Ed had always called her Trina and she wasn't ready for another man to shorten her name. 'Good morning to you, Finlay.'

'Finn. Please. I'm usually Finn. Don't know why I was so formal yesterday.'

'Finn.' She nodded and smiled down at Piper. 'Hello, Piper. What can you see in the rock pool?'

The little girl turned her big green eyes back to the water. Pointed one plump finger. 'Fiss,' Piper said and Finn's eyes widened.

His mouth opened and closed just like the word his daughter had almost mouthed.

'She said fish!' His eyes were alight with wonder and the huge smile on his face made Trina want to hug him to celebrate the moment of pure joy untinged by bitterness. 'I can't believe she said fish.'

'Clever girl,' Trina said and battled not to laugh out loud. She'd thought it had been more like a mumbled *fiss*. But she was sure her father knew better. Her mouth struggled to remain serious. In the end she giggled. Giggled? Again? *What the heck?*

She'd never been a giggler but this guy made her smiles turn into noises she cringed at.

To hide her idiotic response she said, 'I've seen fish too, Piper.'

Finn glanced at her mask. 'You've been snorkelling?'

Trina spread her arms and said with solemn pride, almost dramatically, 'I have been scuba diving.'

'Have you? Go you. I used to love to scuba.' He glanced around. 'Would you like to join us in our pool? There's no lifeguard except me but if you promise not to run or dive we'll let you share.'

Trina scanned the area too. Nobody she knew. She'd look ridiculous, though a voice inside her head said he looked anything but ridiculous in his skin-tight blue rash shirt and board shorts that left not one gorgeous muscle top or bottom unaccounted for.

She put down her mask and the sandals she carried, folded her towel to sit on, hiked up her sundress so it didn't drag in the water and eased herself down at the edge of the pool and put her feet in. The water felt deliciously cool against her suddenly warmer skin.

Finn watched her and she tried not to be aware of that. Then Piper splashed him and the mood broke into something more relaxed. 'So where did you go to scuba?'

She glanced the way she'd come. 'Have you been around the headland?'

He nodded. 'Around the next two until Piper started to feel like a bag of cement on my back.'

Trina laughed. She could so imagine that. She smiled at him. 'The next bay is called Island Bay and the little rocky island that's about four hundred metres out is called Bay Island.'

He laughed. 'Creative people around here.'

She pretended to frown at him. 'I like to think of it as being whimsical.'

'Whimsical. Right.'

She nodded at him. 'Thank you. So, Bay Island is where I did this morning's lesson. Old Tom takes beginners out.'

Piper sat between Finn's legs and he had his big brown long-fingered hands around her tiny waist so she couldn't slip. She was splashing with her starfish hands and silver droplets of water dripped in chasing drops down her father's chest. An unexpected melancholy overwhelmed Trina because the picture made her ache for lost opportunities she should have had with Ed. Opportunities Finn should have had with his wife. She wondered when these thoughts would stop colouring her every experience.

Finn smiled. 'Let me guess. His business is called Old Tom's Dive Shop.'

She jerked back to the present. Her brows crinkled in mock disbelief and she drew the sentence out slowly. 'How did you know that?'

'I'm psychic.' His expression remained serious.

'Really?' She tried for serious too but he was doing it again and her mouth twitched.

'Mmm-hmm. True story.'

'Wow.' She noted the little girl had found a treasure. 'So you can see your daughter is about to put a shell in her mouth?'

Without taking his eyes off Trina's face, his hand came up gently and directed Piper's hand away from her lips. Brushed her fingers open until she dropped the shell and bent down and kissed the little fingers. 'Absolutely.'

'That's fascinating.' And it was. Watching this big bronzed man being so gentle and connected to this tiny girl-child. The bond between them made tears sting Trina's eyes and she pretended she'd splashed water in them.

Until she felt, and heard, her tummy rumble with sullen emptiness and seized on the excuse.

'Well, as lovely as your private ocean pool is, I need to have food. I missed breakfast and I'm starving.'

'Ah. So that's what the noise was,' he teased. 'I thought it was an outboard motor.'

She flicked tiny droplets from her damp fingers at him. 'Too rude.'

He rolled his eyes at her, then shifted Piper from between his legs to sit in the shallow pool and stood up easily. He leant down to offer her his hand. 'Piper's hungry. I should feed her too.'

She barely heard him. His so casually offered fingers were a stumbling block and she hesitated. Piper splashed and she knew she was holding them up. Reluctantly she put out her hand to his and his strong brown fingers closed over hers to lift her smoothly. Way too easily. But the touch of his fingers on hers created such a vibration between them that their eyes met. One pair as startled as the other.

When she was standing he let go quickly and bent down to hoist his daughter into his arms. His face stayed hidden as he tickled her and Trina straightened her own shocked features into a mask of politeness as Piper giggled.

'Well,' she said awkwardly, still rocked by the frisson of awareness that had warmed her whole hand. Her whole arm really. 'Thanks for the swim.'

'Can we walk back with you?'

No, she thought. 'Of course,' she said. And resisted the urge to hold her tingling hand in the other. She bent down and picked up her sandals and mask, slung her towel over her shoulder and resolutely faced the bay until they began walking beside her.

'Would you like to have lunch with us?'

No, she thought. *I can't. I don't know what I'm feeling and it's making me more nervous than scuba diving ever did.* But that was the idea of these new challenges. To challenge things that seemed daunting. And Finn was safe. It took her a long time to answer but strangely she didn't feel pressured to make that snap decision. So she thought about it some more. It was just an impromptu lunch. And Piper made it much easier than if there were just the two of them. 'Okay. Where?'

'How about the beach shop? They have a closed-in play area that Piper loves to crawl around. It's shady and the breeze is always good there.'

'Sounds easy. But how about I meet you there? I didn't bring my purse. I can just run up to the croft and get it.'

He looked a little crestfallen. 'Piper may not last that long. She's nearly ready for her sleep. I could shout you. You could pay for ice creams or something next time?'

Next time? They hadn't tried this time yet. This was all happening way too fast. And wasn't he having as much trouble as she was, putting a toe in the water of opposite sex conversation? Panic built like a wave rising from the ocean to her left. She tried to ride it and not be dumped.

He must have seen the indecision on her face because his features softened in understanding. 'It's okay. We can do a rain-check for another day.'

Disappointment dipped in her stomach. Did she want that? Why was everything so hard? 'No. Let's not. Thank you. I'll just buy the next one, if that's okay. A quick bite would be nice with company.'

They sat under the umbrellas and watched Piper play with a stand of coloured balls, then crawl importantly to steer a pretend ship with a bright blue Captain's wheel. Every time the conversation flagged, Piper sparked a new discussion with some cute little parody of life in her determination to experience all that the colourful play area offered.

Trina could do with her enthusiasm. Considered that fact. 'Babies should be compulsory on all outings. You could watch her all day.'

Finn laughed. Then, more seriously, said, 'I do. She keeps me sane. Makes me get out of bed in the morning.'

Trina knew that feeling. 'Well, you've certainly been busy since you got here. Your cottage is pretty in pink.'

'Piper chose the colour,' he said and then looked at her as if expecting her to laugh.

'So she's a pink girl. I can believe that. It looks good on her.' Trina rested her cheek on her hand to watch his face, trying to understand why he should be so wary. 'How did you get her to choose?'

'I gave her swatches. I was hoping for blue but she took the pink every time.'

Too funny. Trina laughed. 'Great idea. I can see that too.' She looked at his face and his beautiful smile. She shook her head. 'Her decision. You were stuck with it. Nothing you can do about that, then.'

He shrugged, his expression light and relaxed. It made her warm that he could be that way around her. 'I'm used to it now. I've been learning to be a handyman. And quite enjoying the challenge.'

Handyman. Or woman. The bane of her life. She rolled her eyes. 'Boy, have I had some repair challenges in the last two years? I've had to learn that too. Maybe I should paint my croft. Just yesterday I was thinking it looks very dark inside.' She shut her mouth. Now, why did she say that? Almost an invitation for help.

Finn's voice was light—lighter than her thoughts. 'I can send Piper up if you like. To talk colours with you.'

Trina felt herself relax. He got it. Her expression had probably telegraphed the message that she'd regretted being so open. 'I might take you up on that one day.' She could hear the relief in her voice. Hoped he couldn't.

They'd finished their roast beef sandwiches

and iced coffee and Trina desperately needed some distance to think about the morning with Finn but the moment passed.

A commotion at the next table made them both turn. A woman had overturned her chair and the crash turned every head her way. She shook a small child hysterically. 'Spit it out. Come on.' She glanced around wildly. 'He swallowed a button.'

The child gasped weakly, tried to cry and couldn't find enough air to do so as he gulped and coughed. His face was tinged an alarming shade of blue as his mouth quivered.

Finn rose from their table and crossed the space in two strides. 'May I? I'm a doctor.' He didn't wait long.

The woman sagged, nodded and, sobbing in panic, watched as Finn took the child from her. Trina had followed him and righted the woman's chair and urged her back into it. Finn was a doctor. *Wow.* He'd said he wasn't a vet.

Finn sank into the nearest seat and lay the little boy, head down, across his knees and patted his mid back firmly in slow pats.

Trina leaned towards him. 'Can I help?'

Finn shook his head and concentrated on

the boy. He patted again, then tipped him further. 'Come on now, mate. Everything is fine. Cough it up.'

To Trina's relief a sudden plop heralded the arrival of the button as it flew out onto the floor, initiating a collective sigh of relief from the entire café. And her. *Wow. Calmness is us.*

Finn righted the little boy and gave him a reassuring squeeze. Then he stood up with the exhausted child in his arms and passed him to his mother as if nothing had happened.

'He'll be fine. Just needs a minute to get his breath back.' He rested his hand on her shoulder and spoke quietly into her ear. Trina couldn't hear what he said but the woman nodded. Once. Twice. Glanced at the boy in her arms and squeezed him tighter. Then looked back at Finn with a vehement nod. 'Thank you.' The words were heartfelt.

Trina felt her eyes sting. Her heart still thudded from the spectre of a child choking to death in front of them all. She had no doubt everyone there had felt for the fear of the mother, though Trina would have liked to have given her a few pointers about first aid manoeuvres.

She glanced to where Piper played contentedly, oblivious to the drama she'd missed, and oblivious to the fact her daddy had quite possibly just saved a little boy's life. Trina wanted to go home. She felt too emotional to be out in public. Though she suspected she would still be thinking about Finn even if she was away from him.

When Finn sat back down and the conversations around them had begun again she nodded towards the woman, who was paying her bill and leaving with her little boy hugging her leg as he waited.

'Good job. What did you say to her?' She didn't mention he'd said he was a doctor. It didn't matter what he was.

'I asked if she'd seen what I did and, if there was a next time, to try that instead. That shaking didn't help and was actually dangerous. That calm speaking would relax the oesophagus as well.'

'I'm impressed. Discreet and direct.' The guy did everything right. But she still needed to get away from the emotionally charged atmosphere. She collected her mask and towel from the ground beside her and pushed her chair back. 'Before all the excitement I was about to leave. So thank you for lunch.' She glanced at his daughter, who had apparently wrung every conceivable amusement out of the play area and looked to be ready to depart as well.

'Maybe next weekend I could repay the favour.' Piper wailed. 'As long as Piper is free?'

Finn stood up to rescue his daughter. 'I'll look in her calendar and let you know.'

Their eyes connected for a moment, both a little bemused by the ease of their conversation. 'That would be lovely. Thank you, Finn.'

'Thank you, Catrina.' He watched her again and she knew he didn't want her to go. His approval circled her like a whisper of flame crackling and warming her around the base of her lost confidence. But the lure of time away from this new and challenging situation beckoned enticingly.

She stood and waved to the tiny girl. 'Bye, Piper.'

CHAPTER SEVEN

Finn

FINN WATCHED HER walk swiftly across the car park to the path. Almost hurrying away from him. Was it the incident with the little boy? That had turned out okay. Poor terrified little kid and mum—but all right now.

His eyes followed Catrina as Piper leaned into his neck. Maybe she'd left because she felt he was pushing for her company? He was. Why was he pressuring her? If someone had pushed him like he was pushing her he'd have run for the hills. Or a croft. Which she did.

Maybe he was sabotaging himself and hoping she'd stop it before he did? But there was no getting over the fact he'd been a little desperate for Catrina to stay.

And then there had been that jolt when he'd helped her stand at the rock pool. Unconsciously his hands came together to replicate the action, as if to see if he could still feel that vibration that had taken them both by surprise. It had been bizarre, and he'd seen the shock in her face—apparently he hadn't been the only one to feel it—before he'd picked up Piper to give himself a moment to recover.

He wished he'd told her it was Piper's birthday tomorrow. Because at lunch, after an initial stiffness, conversation had felt so easy. It had been strangely healing to have her sitting opposite him as they both watched his baby playing. When Catrina was there it was easier not to think about where Piper's mother would be tomorrow.

The guilt hit him like a fist in the chest and he sucked in his breath. What was he doing? How could he think that? He was a coward and tomorrow he'd celebrate Piper— he needed to be man enough not to cower in a corner feeling sorry for himself. He paid the bill and gathered Piper up in his arms.

Tomorrow he'd survive and Monday he'd see about getting a job.

Sunday morning Finn woke with a headache. Unusually, Piper had been unsettled most of the night and he wondered if they were both coming down with a cold. Or if the emotion of the coming anniversary of Clancy's desertion was rubbing off him and onto Piper.

He took two paracetamol and a vitamin tablet, and hand-squeezed an orange to give Piper with her breakfast. Because she was still asleep, he decided they wouldn't go out for the day if they were both unwell. He looked at the two wrapped presents he had for Piper. One was a tiny gardening set in a flower-decorated garden basket and the other a push-along block set for inside or out.

The cupboard above the sink drew his eyes and he crossed the room and searched for the packet cake mix he'd thrown in there a month ago in case he needed to make Piper's birthday cake. The packet mix came with little blue cupcake wrappers, pink frosting and fairy princess stickers to press into the icing after they'd been cooked.

The instructions seemed basic and he set it all out, with the candle, for later when he could make some noise. He glanced across at Piper but she snored gently and he wandered to the front of the beach house and stared out at the waves across the bay.

He could see Catrina walking along the

breakwall and watched her brisk walk as she strode further away, the wind whipping her hair across her face. He wanted to wave and call her and share the burden and the blessing of this day with her, but knew he wouldn't.

'Last thing she needs,' he told himself out loud, keeping his voice quiet.

'Boo,' said a little voice from behind him and he turned to see Piper standing in her cot with her bunny cuddle blanket over her face.

Despite his aching heart, he smiled. 'Where's Piper?'

Piper pulled the blanket off her head and appeared like magic. Her eyes crinkled with delight at her own cleverness. 'Boo.'

'There she is.' He crossed the room to her but before he arrived he put his hands over his face and then pulled them away. 'Boo to you too, missy. Happy birthday, Piper!' He lifted her up out of her cot and hugged her. She gurgled with squirming delight and he had to force himself not to squeeze her too tight.

He began to sing 'Happy birthday' but faltered halfway through when he thought of Clancy and all she was missing. Forcing himself to finish the song, he carried Piper over to the window. 'It's a breezy sunny day for your birthday. What would you like to do?'

Piper put her head on his shoulder and snuggled in.

Suddenly it was okay again. They could do this. 'You feeling a little fragile today, poppet? Me too. But I'm making you a cake this morning. You can help by pushing on the stickers. It will be our first cake but your daddy is a doctor and supposed to be very smart. I'm sure we can manage little pink cakes for our birthday girl.' She bounced with a little more enthusiasm in his arms.

'Then we can sit outside and let the sunshine and fresh air kill all the germs, if there are any. No work today. Lazy day.'

He put Piper down on the floor and she crawled away from him to her box of toys in the corner with just a little less than her usual surprising speed.

He watched her go and thought about looking for childcare tomorrow. If he couldn't find anything then they'd leave it all for a while longer. That thought brought comfort. Surely it would be hard to find someone in a small town like this at such short notice.

He glanced out of the window again down

to the beach and saw Catrina was on her way
back. She didn't pass his house, or hadn't in
the past or he would have noticed, and he
leaned towards the window and saw her
moving up the hill towards the cliff opposite
the lighthouse. She'd said 'croft' yesterday.
Maybe she was in one of those three little
cottages on the cliffs that matched the lighthouse. All white stone.

He'd liked the look of them but the real estate agent had said they weren't for sale. He'd
never actually gone up that way towards the
hospital along the cliff path. Maybe it would
be a nice place to go for a change when he
went walking with Piper. Just in case he was
missing out on a good walk, he reassured
himself. But not today. He had promised he'd
never drop in uninvited and had no intention
of doing so.

Except the morning dragged. They went
to the beach but the wind was a little cool to
get wet and if Piper was coming down with
a cold he didn't want to make it worse. Before long they went home and played inside.
But he felt closed in staying indoors. Piper
seemed to have recovered and before lunch
she'd become unusually bored.

So after lunch, full from eating little pink cakes and with a sealed bag holding an extra one, he hefted Piper onto his back and went for a walk up the hill.

Yes, he nodded to himself dryly, towards the cliff path, not totally directed to one of the crofts that he wondered might belong to Catrina, but certainly it felt good to be outside, with a fresh breeze blowing the cobwebs and fingers of darkness from his lowered mood.

'Dad, Dad, Dad,' Piper burbled from behind his ear—so Piper liked being outside too, and it was her birthday. He was supposed to be doing what she wanted. Each of his steps up the hill lightened his mood and the hill path was well maintained and solid under his feet. He could feel the exertion and decided Catrina could probably run up this hill if she did it a couple of times a day. He wasn't quite up to that yet.

The path forked towards the cottages one way and down onto a cliff edge path on the other and he realised the crofts had hedges around them for privacy from below.

That was good. He wouldn't want anybody to be able to peek into Catrina's house just by walking along the path, but it was a tiny bit disappointing that he couldn't see any of the buildings up close. Then he rounded a bend and the path snaked up again and as he trekked up the hill he realised they'd come out past the cottages.

Quite ingenious really. At the top they came out onto a little open area with a bench and an ancient telescope that had been cemented into the footpath to look out to sea.

He paused and bent down to peer through it, which was hard with Piper suddenly excited and bouncing on his back, when a voice spoke behind him.

'I bet Piper is heavier going uphill.'

He could feel the smile on his face as he turned— he hadn't imagined her.

'Hello there, Catrina.'

'Hello, you two, and what are you doing up here in the clouds?'

'We've never been here before. And it's Piper's birthday.'

Her face broke into a shining sunbeam of a smile and she stepped closer to drop a kiss on Piper's cheek. 'Happy birthday, sweetheart. I hope Daddy made you a cake.'

Piper bounced and crowed.

'Of course. Though really we made cup-cakes with pink princess stickers.'

This time the smile was for him. 'I wish I could have seen them.'

It felt good to know he'd thought ahead. 'By a stroke of luck, we do have a spare one in our bag which I'm sure Piper would love to share with you?' He looked around and considered the logistics of Piper and a cliff edge. Maybe not.

It seemed that Catrina got it in one. 'It's too tricky here for a birthday girl. Come back and I'll show you the croft. We can sit on the balcony; it's well fenced and safe.'

CHAPTER EIGHT

Trina

TRINA TURNED ON the path and directed them along the other fork back towards her house, beckoning them to follow. Thankfully, facing the other way, Finn couldn't see the expression on her face. She still couldn't believe she'd invited them into her home. So blithely. Since when had her bravery suddenly known no bounds?

Well, she could hear Finn's springing footsteps behind her as she led the way around the loop that led to the cottages again and within seconds they'd popped out onto the road outside the last croft, where Myra and Dr Southwell lived. As they passed the door opened and the older gentleman stepped out.

He smiled when he saw her, and then his face lit up further when he saw who followed her. 'Trina. And Finn. And Piper. Hello. Delightful. So, you've met.'

Trina could feel herself blush. 'Hello. Yes. At the beach.' Glancing around for inspiration to change the subject, she added, 'Lovely day.' Not only had she invited a man back to her house but she'd been caught in the act. Everyone would know. Dr Southwell wasn't a gossip but, seriously, Ellie's father-in-law? *Small blinkin' towns.*

Trina blushed again under Dr Southwell's pleased smile.

'The weather is super. Love to stay and chat but I'm off to the hospital.' He waved and strode off.

Trina shrugged off the awkwardness with determination. 'So that's who lives next door on this side and my boss, Ellie, and her husband, who happens to be an obstetrician, Dr Southwell's son, live on the other side.'

He looked around at the three crofts as they came to hers, and paused. 'You're well covered for medical help then.' He smiled a little awkwardly.

'Never too many in an emergency.' She smiled back, too concerned with whether she'd left the house tidy before he arrived to worry about trying to read his reaction to her neighbours. She indicated her own front path. 'Come in. It's small but compact, much like yours is, I imagine.'

'Yes. Tiny, but I like it. You'll have to come and see my renovations.'

Not your etchings? She thought it and smiled to herself. Didn't risk saying anything in case he heard the amusement in her voice. At least she could be amused by something that she would have run a mile from a month ago. In fact, she could have rubbed her knuckles on her chest. Darn proud of herself, really.

She pushed open the door and was glad she'd opened all the blinds this morning. With everything open the sea seemed to be a part of the room, with all eyes being drawn to the open French windows out onto the little terrace. She gestured him to walk that way.

'Great view,' Finn said after a low whistle. 'That's really magic.' He walked slowly to the French windows and absently began to undo Piper's straps.

Trina came up behind him and undid the other one. 'Here, let me help.' She lifted Piper out of the straps and set her down. 'There's nothing to climb on. I only keep the swing chair out there and it's against the house wall. It has to come in when it's windy.'

Piper crawled straight for the rails and her little hands grabbed on as she pulled herself up. She bounced on the balls of her feet. Finn followed her out and Trina stood back a little and admired them both.

A bouncy, healthy little girl and her gorgeous dad. She wasn't sure when he'd graduated from attractive to other women to gorgeous for her, but she had to admit he made an admirable picture with his big shoulders and strong back silhouetted against the ocean. His long fingers rested lightly and then the curved muscles in his arms bunched as he gripped the rail for a minute. She wondered what he was thinking about as he stood guard over his daughter, his powerful thighs either side of her as one hand left the rail and brushed her small head.

Then the penny dropped. Piper's birthday. And his wife had left soon after Piper's birth. That made this time of year a distressing anniversary as well as a day for celebration for Piper. Tough call. She hadn't even crawled out of bed on the anniversary of losing Ed.

Why hadn't he said something yesterday?

Then she chastised herself. Why would he share that with a stranger?

She swallowed past the lump that had suddenly formed in her throat. 'Would you two like a cold drink?' She managed to even her voice. 'I have a spill-proof cup I use for one of my friend's daughters.'

'Piper has her water here, thanks.' He came back in and bent down to Piper's pack. Pulled out a little pink pop-top bottle. 'She'll use hers.' Then he pulled out a Ziploc bag. 'Aha! Here's your part of Piper's birthday cake.'

He glanced back at his daughter. 'Probably best she doesn't see it as I had no idea she could gobble as many as she did and she'll be sick if she eats any more.'

Trina nodded and swiped the bag, turning her back to the veranda and opening the seal. She lifted out the little blue-papered cake and admired the rough pink icing and slightly off-centre sticker. 'It's magnificent.'

'Piper put the stickers on herself.'

'Clever girl.' She looked at him. 'Clever Daddy for the rest.'

He looked at her. Maybe saw the lingering distress in her eyes and he closed his own for a minute and then looked at her again. Nodded. 'So you've guessed it's a tough day?'

'You have a different set of triggers but I was just thinking I didn't even get out of bed when mine went past.' They needed to get out and fill the day with something. 'How about we go for a walk along the cliffs further? There's a really cool cave overlooking the ocean about a kilometre north I could show you. And there's a sweet little dip of green grass Piper would love.' She smiled at the thought. 'She could probably log roll down the tiny hill. I watched some kids do that one day and it looked fun.'

She saw relief lift the creases from his brow. 'That does sound good. Is there somewhere you'd prefer me to change Piper before we go? I have a change mat.'

'You have everything!' And wasn't that true. 'Change mats are great. You can use my bed and save you bending down. I'll make a little snack for the meadow.' She turned away. Excited for the first time in a long while with a task she couldn't wait to play with.

She slipped in two small cans of mixer cordial that she'd bought on a whim. A packet of dates and apricots for Piper. She even had arrowroot biscuits, perfect for a little girl to make a mess with. Threw in some crisps, two apples and a banana. It all fitted in her little cool bag she carried to work each day, along with the tiny checked throw she had never had the opportunity to use for a picnic.

They set off ten minutes later, Piper bouncing on her daddy's back and Trina swinging along beside them as if she was a part of the little family. She winced at her instinctive comparison. No. Like a party of friends. Looking out for each other.

The sun shone clear and warm on their backs as they strode along the path. The sea breeze blew Piper's bright golden mist of hair around her chubby face as she chattered away. Trina decided Finn looked so much more relaxed out in the open. It made her feel good that she'd helped.

A cruise ship hugged the horizon and she pointed it out to Finn. Piper saw a seabird dive into the water far below and they had to stop and watch for a minute until it came out again with a fish in its beak.

Trina admired the skill of the surfers, bobbing and swooping like brilliant supple-bodied flying fish on the curling waves.

When she commented, Finn shared, 'I love surfing.'

'I've never tried.' Maybe she could add that to her adventure list.

Finn said, 'When Piper is old enough I'll teach her to surf. This looks a great place to do that.'

'Dr Southwell used to surf every morning before he was married. Though I have to admit he did come a cropper when he was washed off the shelf last year.'

He looked back the way they'd come. 'Really? Ouch. Which shelf?'

She pointed. 'The ones under the cliffs, with the rock pools we were in yesterday.'

Finn frowned. 'It doesn't look dangerous there.'

'It is on a king tide. And his timing was off if you ask him. They lifted him out with a chopper but the good news was his son met Ellie, my boss, when he came to locum while his father was away, and they married and are having a baby. That's why I'm doing Ellie's job for the next year—hence the change from night duty.'

'Happy ending.' His voice held only a trace

of bitterness. She got that. But she'd moved on herself, thankfully.

She wondered if he'd heard his own subtext because his voice came out warmer than before. 'So were they all the people in the restaurant on Friday?'

She'd forgotten. 'Yes, that's right—you were there. With Piper and your sister.' She thought back over those present. 'They were celebrating Ellie's leave and my promotion.'

'Congratulations.'

She laughed. 'Thanks. First day tomorrow. We'll see.'

She thought back to Friday and the pleasant lunch. Her own surprise to see Finn there. With another woman. Felt just a little embarrassed now she knew it was his sister. Hurried on in case it showed on her face. 'The other older lady at the table is the one who makes the most divine cakes—Dr Southwell's wife, Myra.'

'I guess I'll get to know them all. Dr Southwell's offered me a place in his practice. I'll start as soon as I can find day care for Piper.'

She raised her brows. 'Do you have a specialty?'

'I started in general practice. Then I went

on and studied paediatrics. I thought everyone knew?' Then he shook his head. 'I guess I haven't really spoken to many people. I have my Diploma of Obstetrics from my GP days, but no real experience in that. Just the antenatal side of it. Not the delivery part.'

He didn't look old enough to have done all that. Catrina smiled at him, decided she wouldn't share that thought and shook her head mockingly. 'We don't say delivery any more. Especially in Lighthouse Bay. We're Midwifery Group Practice.'

He put his hands up. 'Midwifery Group Practice. And I said *delivery*. My bad.'

'Very.' She smiled at him. 'Everything is midwifery-led and woman-centred. The antenatal clinic is drop-in and popular. When the mother births, we support her choice to stay or go, and she's visited at home within the day after if that's what she wants or she can stay for a few days in the hospital. Either way, we don't call a doctor unless someone is sick.'

He put out his hands helplessly and pretended to sigh. 'I'm defunct and I haven't even started.'

She laughed. 'You'll get used to it. You should meet Ellie and her husband. Sam's the

Director of Obstetrics at the base hospital and fell in love with Lighthouse Bay too. And Ellie, of course.' She smiled at the thought. 'Sam moved here from a big Brisbane Hospital so we're lucky to have him as an unofficial back-up in real emergencies when he's not on-call at the base hospital.'

She looked at him thoughtfully. 'I've thought of someone who could mind Piper, if you're interested.'

His face went blank and she hesitated. Maybe he wasn't ready yet.

'I'll need to find someone eventually,' he managed but she could see it cost him. She wished she hadn't mentioned it now.

Then he said more firmly, 'Sure. That would be great. I need to start looking.'

Trina thought about Marni. She didn't regret mentioning her, though. 'She's a doll. A natural mother. Her twins are six months old and she's just registered for day care status.'

CHAPTER NINE

Finn

FINN FELT HIS stomach drop. He wasn't seeing the path or the ocean or the sky overhead.
He shouldn't have asked about day care. But
something inside had dared him to. Something that wanted him to move on, as if he'd
known he'd be catapulted into a decision if
he put it out there. All his instincts wanted to
draw back. Stop her telling him. Say he'd ask
if he decided it was time. She'd understand.
Not sure how he knew that but he believed
in the truth of it.

Instead he said, 'Would you recommend
her?'

She looked at him thoughtfully. Kindly.
'That's tough because it's not about me,' she
said gently, as if she could read his distress.
Then she looked at Piper. 'Marni could mind

my child, if I had one.' The tone was almost joking. He saw something that looked like pain flit across her face and remembered again there were people out there who did suffer as much as he did. People like Catrina. Left alone by the love of their life—without choice and unintentionally. Loss of love and no baby to hold like he did. Imagine life without Piper.

Catrina's voice wasn't quite steady but he could hear the struggle to make it so. It had been a very brave thing to say and he wanted to tell her that. Wanted to tell her that he understood. But still the coward inside him shied away from so much emotion.

Catrina said, 'Maybe you could see if Piper likes her before you commit to work and see how she goes? Just an hour or two?'

'That's a good idea. Tell me about her.'

He saw her gaze into the distance, a soft smile on her face and a glimmer of distress, though this time he didn't think it was for herself. 'She's a younger mum. Early twenties. She and her husband own the dry-cleaners in town but she's a stay-at-home mum. Marni's Mother Earth and the boys are six months old. Bundles of energy, healthy as all get-out, which is great because she nearly lost them at twenty-three weeks, and she spent a lot of time in hospital. As far as the midwives of Lighthouse Bay think, she's a hero to us.'

He had to smile at that. '*The Midwives of Lighthouse Bay*. Sounds like a serial on TV.'

She laughed a little self-consciously and he regretted making light of the one stable thing she had in her life, hadn't meant to embarrass her. 'Don't get me wrong. It's another good ending to a story.'

Catrina seemed to relax. 'It really was. Ellie's husband, Sam, had been involved in research into preventing extreme premature birth in Brisbane, and thankfully he was here when she went into labour. Marni and Bob are a lovely couple who'd already lost an extremely premature baby daughter.'

Finn wasn't so sure. She already had twins and he wanted someone who could concentrate on Piper. 'How could she care for Piper as well?' Finn was more uncertain now. 'Sounds a bit hectic. She has twins and she's doing day care?'

He caught Trina's encouraging smile and suddenly saw how she could be a good midwife. Her empathy shone warm—he felt she understood and was reassuring him that he would conquer his fear of letting Piper out of his sight. All without putting on pressure. Encouraging him to test his own strength without expectations. Treating him like a woman in labour battling her own fear. *Wow*. She had it down pat.

Then she said, 'She loves minding babies. And babies love her. Usually she's minding them for free. We keep telling her she should become a midwife and I wouldn't be surprised when the boys go to school if she'll look at it. But, for now, she's just starting up official day care.'

Absently he bent and stroked Piper's leg at his side. 'Maybe I could meet her before I talk to Dr Southwell? It's a good idea to see if Piper likes her before I commit to work, though. You'll have to give me her number.'

'Or we could visit her. Meet her and her husband. See their house. They're a lovely couple and live only a few doors up from you. In the blue pastel cottage.'

It was all happening too quickly. He could feel the panic build and squashed it down again. He could do this. Just not today.

Catrina touched his arm—the first time

she had physically connected with him of her own volition—and again that frisson of awareness hummed where they touched. He glanced at her but her expression still showed only compassionate support. 'It's something to think about. Marni is just the one I know. There will be others when you're ready.'

His relief made his shoulders sag. She must have seen it on his face. Was he that transparent? He'd have to work on his game face before he went back to work or his patients' parents would run a mile.

He tried to make light of it. 'I imagine every parent must feel like this when they have to go back to work. Torn.'

'Absolutely. We see mums that can't stay in hospital for one night after birth because they hate leaving the other child or children too much.' She looked towards Piper and smiled. 'I'd find it hard to leave Piper if she were mine.'

His face tightened. He could feel it. Some women could. Piper's mother had no problem. And he'd be the one who had to break his daughter's heart when the time came to tell the truth.

Catrina opened her mouth—he didn't want

to talk about Clancy—but all she said was,
'The cave's just around this next headland.'
He was glad she'd changed the subject.

The cave, when they arrived, curved back
into the cliff and created an overhang half the
size of his house. A few round boulders acted
as seats for looking out over the ocean out of
the sun. Or rain. Plenty of evidence suggested
people had camped and made campfires there
but on the whole it had stayed clean and cool,
and dim towards the back. The sort of place
young boys would love to go with their mates.

He could stand up in the cave easily and
they stomped around in it for a few minutes
before Catrina suggested they go the small
distance further to the glade so Piper could
be released from the backpack.

The glade, when they arrived, had a park
bench and table at the edge of the slope
down into the bowl-shaped dip of grass. The
bright sunshine made the grass lime cordial-
coloured and the thick bed of kikuyu and dai-
sies felt softer and springier than he expected
when he put Piper down to crawl. Because of
the sloping sides of the bowl Piper tended to
end up back in the lowest point in the middle even when she climbed the sides and he

could feel his mouth twitching as she furrowed her brows and tried to work out what was happening.

He pulled a bright saucer-sized ball from her backpack and tossed it in the centre of the glade while Catrina set their picnic bag on the table and spread the cloth. Piper crawled to the ball and batted it. Of course it rolled back down the side to her again. She pushed it again and crowed when it rolled back again.

'Clever girl,' he said to his daughter, and 'Clever girl,' to Catrina, who grinned at him as she finished laying out their treats and came to sit next to him on the side of the grass hill. 'I can't remember when I last had a picnic,' he said as he passed an arrowroot biscuit to Piper and took one of the apples for himself.

'I know. Me either.' She handed him the can of drink and took a sip of her own. Then he heard her sigh blissfully.

'We couldn't have had more beautiful weather this afternoon.'

'A bit different to this morning.'

'That's the beauty of Lighthouse Bay. We're temperate. Not too hot for long or too cold for long. Always leaning towards perfect weather.'

'Always?'

Catrina laughed. 'Well, no. We do have wild storms sometimes. That's why I have shutters on my windows and doors. But not often.'

The afternoon passed in a desultory fashion and once, when Piper dozed off in his arms, he and Catrina lay side by side watching the clouds pass overhead in companionable silence. He'd never met anyone as restful as she was. It would have been so simple to slide closer and take her hand but the man who could have done that had broken a year ago.

An hour later, on the way home from their walk, he asked again about the exact location of the day care mum.

'I could come with you to knock on the door? Maybe meeting the family would help?'

'Just drop in?' Despite his initial reluctance, he could see that an impromptu visit could be less orchestrated than one when they expected him. And he had Catrina to come with him to break the ice.

It made sense. Not fair perhaps, but this

was his baby he was considering leaving in their care, and he wanted a true representation of the feeling of the household.

When the door opened to answer his knock, a smiling red-haired man answered. Past him they could hear the sound of a child squealing and the smell of a roast dinner drifted out to tantalise his nose. He hadn't had an old-fashioned roast for years. His mouth watered.

'Can I help you?' Then the man saw Catrina and smiled beatifically. 'Trina!'

'Hello, Bob. How are you?' The man stepped forward and hugged her and Finn was surprised.

When they stepped back from each other she said, 'Something smells divine. Lucky you—Sunday roast.'

'You're welcome any time, Trina.' He grinned and looked at her companion.

'This is Finn Foley. He's a friend and I told him about Marni offering childcare and—' she indicated Piper '—he and Piper have just started looking.' Finn glanced at Catrina. Took a second to savour that she'd claimed friendship. She really was his only friend here.

She still spoke to Bob. 'I wondered if he could have a chat with Marni?'

'Absolutely. Any friend of yours and all that.' Bob grinned at Finn. 'Come in. Marni? There's a dad here looking for information about childcare.'

Finn liked the way he said that. To his wife, with deference, and that he wasn't committing to anything. Just asking. His nerves settled a fraction as he followed Catrina, with Piper on his back, in the door.

The room had been divided into two, with a kitchen and lounge on one side and a wall with doors on the other. Bedrooms, he guessed, unlike his one-room cottage. An extension had been built out the back with a big play room that overlooked the tiny fenced garden. Everything sparkled; even the toys strewn on the floor in the play room caught the sunlight and looked new and well cared for. The family warmth in the little abode made the tension drop from his shoulders and his eyes met Trina's in acknowledgement.

A young woman crossed to them, drying her hands on a tea towel. She too hugged Catrina, and her shy smile eased the tension in

Finn's stomach like magic. 'Trina. Great to see you.'

'This is Finn, Marni.' She turned to help Finn extricate Piper from the backpack—which he was pretty darn good at, but he had to admit it was quicker with help. And he liked her touching him.

'Nice to meet you, Finn. You live a few doors down, don't you?' she said as she held out her hand. They shook briefly and he liked that her fingers were cool and dry, her grip confident.

'Welcome.' She smiled at Piper, who now sat on his hip, then turned around and pointed to two boys as if introducing her to them not Finn. 'The one on the left is Olly, and the cheekier one is Mikey.' She looked at Piper. 'And what is your name, beautiful?'

Previously fascinated by the smaller humans, Piper looked back at the lady's face, realised everyone was looking at her and then she clutched at his neck and buried her face.

Finn rubbed her back. 'Piper can be shy.'

'Of course she can.' Marni indicated the rear of the cottage. 'Come and sit out on the deck at the back and we'll show you the play area and I can answer your questions.

'So Catrina told you I've started doing childcare?' The smile Marni gave Catrina lit up her face. 'The midwives are my cheer squad. They're all champions up there. If it wasn't for them and the younger Dr Southwell, we wouldn't have our gorgeous boys.'

Finn looked at the two chubby-faced little boys, one sitting in a blue tub of a chair kicking his feet and the other lying on his back on the patterned play carpet with a red spiral rattle. The little boy—Finn thought it was Olly—began to screw his face up, dropped the rattle and began to rock until he rolled over and lay on his stomach. The mischievous chortle he let out at the feat made Finn smile.

'Clever boy, Mikey,' his dad said. So he'd got that wrong, Finn thought. And then Bob gestured to his wife. 'I'll finish the potatoes. You take our guests and Piper out and have a chat.'

Finn liked that too. He could see they were a team and, despite having two babies, the air of serenity as Marni smiled made his trepidations settle. This sort of calm atmosphere looked perfect for Piper to learn about other babies and new adults.

A heck of a lot different to the busy, efficient childcare he'd had her in before. But Piper still clung to him like one of the stripy shells on the side of a rock pool and he remembered the hard times at the big kindergarten when he'd tried to leave.

Marni pointed to a scrubbed wooden table and four sturdy chairs. Two highchairs took up the other spaces. They all sat down and Marni put a soft-sided squeaky farm book on the table in front of Piper without making a fuss of it.

'I am looking for two more toddlers. That will give me enough to cover the wage of the girl working with my husband at the dry-cleaners and then there's no rush for me to go back to work. I'm hoping to stay home for the next year at least. In a perfect world, I won't go back to work until the boys go to school.'

She smiled calmly at Finn. 'But we'll see what happens.'

So a stable place, Finn was thinking, and he wondered, if he offered to pay twice the rate, would Marni consider having Piper by herself, at least at the beginning so the young mum wasn't pushed by the demands of four children? Piper would benefit and money wasn't a problem. Finding someone caring and kind for Piper would be priceless.

He tried to think of a question. 'Catrina said you've just been registered. Having two babies seems intense to me. Piper can keep me busy and there's only one of her.'

She glanced lovingly towards the two gurgling on the floor and then across at her husband. 'I mind lots of children. Have always loved them and thought for a while we'd never be able to have any. But then the boys came along, though I spent a couple of months in hospital hanging onto them, so they are beyond precious.'

She shrugged ruefully. 'I'm worried I might spoil them and want them to learn to share, not just with each other but with other children. Some extra income would help and my husband and I are both the eldest from big families. Our families are in Western Australia so we miss having lots of kids around.'

'I guess childminding makes sense in that case.'

Piper reached out and picked up the book. Scrunched it with her inquisitive fingers. Barely audible squeaks erupted when she squeezed and a crooked smile tipped her mouth as she battled between shyness and delight.

All the adults looked at her fondly. 'So, information-wise, what sort of minding were you looking for?'

'I've been offered a position three days a week, Monday, Tuesday and Wednesday.'

Marni nodded. 'Three is better than five for Piper. Especially in the beginning. Has she been in care before?'

'Yes, poor baby, most of her life, when I worked. About fifty hours a week. But not for the last six weeks and she was becoming unhappy before that. I was thinking to start a half-day, as a trial, just until Piper gets used to it. If she gets too upset I'd probably not go back to work for a while.' He shrugged his apology.

Apparently she didn't need it. That serene smile drifted across her face. 'Being adaptable is good around kids. One of the secrets. She'll miss you if she's had you to herself for six weeks.' A quirked brow made that question.

'I'm not even sure it's what I'm ready to do.'

'That's fine. You're fact-finding, which is very sensible.'

Well, he'd better glean some facts. This was harder than he'd thought it would be. He glanced at Catrina and she sat tranquilly beside him, lending moral support, not interrupting. Just there. It felt good not to be on his own through this. 'What hours do you have available?'

Marni laughed. 'As I haven't started yet it's hard to say. Big picture—Monday to Friday, no more than forty hours, but the hours are flexible. And I get to keep the weekends for the boys and Bob.'

'Where would she sleep in the daytime?'

'We've a little room next to the boys' room. Bob put two new folding cots in there and I think it'll work well. And I'll supply all the food. No hardship to make for one more and that way nobody wants what others have.'

It all sounded too good to be true. Plus they lived a few doors away from his own house. Even in this short time Piper seemed relaxed here. He gently swung her off his lap, book still in her hands, and rested her bottom on the floor. Just to see if she'd go.

As soon as she hit the floor she dropped the book and crawled curiously towards the two little boys. Stopped about a body's length away and sat up. The three tiny people all looked at each other.

The adults smiled and Finn felt the tension leave his shoulders. The gods, or Catrina, had saved him again.

'What about if I go and talk to my prospective employer tomorrow? Perhaps leave Piper here just for an hour and see how she goes while I negotiate? Then we'll all know more.'

'Why don't you make it two hours? That will be a quarter of the time of her next visit, if you decide to go ahead. Just to give her time to settle. And take the rush out of your appointment. She'll be fine. It will give us all a chance to trial the fit.'

'I think that sounds like a plan. Yes, please.' Finn stood up. Blew out a breath. 'Phew. Thank you. I do feel better for asking and talking to you. That would be great.' He glanced at Catrina, who stood as well. She smiled at him as if he'd just done an excellent job. It felt good. Reassuring.

Marni went across to the dresser and picked up a business card. 'Here's our phone number, and it's got my mobile on it as well. You can ring or drop in when you know your time. The sheet has information about my business.' She handed him a sheet of paper with her numbers and the payment rates. Easy.

'That's great.' He picked up Piper, who had crawled over to him as soon as he stood up. She didn't cling, more curious than panicked he'd leave her. 'I'll leave one of my own cards when I bring Piper. Then you can contact me any time.'

'Give yourself ten extra minutes before you leave her tomorrow. To help her settle.'

He nodded. Then Bob came and shook his hand. Then they were outside and the door closed.

He felt like sagging against it. He'd done it. Another step towards a new life.

'You didn't say much.'

Catrina laughed. 'I didn't have to. You're all made for each other.'

CHAPTER TEN

Trina

TRINA'S FIRST MORNING as Midwifery Unit Manager, and her first day shift for a long time, proved too busy to worry about a man she'd met on the beach and declared her friend. Though she had spent a fair time mulling over all the things she'd learnt about Finn the night before.

This morning, in her new world, the midwife coming off shift had celebrated a birth at five a.m., so still lots of settling of mother and baby for Trina to help with before mother left at lunchtime to go home. Another mother who preferred to rest at home, not separated from her toddler, and it made her think of her conversation with Finn yesterday. Finn again. She pushed those thoughts away and concentrated on the new tasks.

There were Monday pharmacy orders and sterile stock orders, and a hospital meeting and a visit from Myra, her neighbour, which lightened a busy time with a quick break.

'Hello there, new midwife in charge.' Myra's serene face peered around the corner of the nurses' station, where Trina typed efficiently into the discharged mother's electronic medical records.

'Hello, Mrs Southwell, what have you got there?' Myra had a steaming cup and a white paper bag tucked under her arm. Ellie had said that Myra always brought something when the place got busy.

'A long black with extra water, the way you like it.' She smiled mischievously. 'And a savoury tart with spring onion in case you haven't had lunch.'

Trina glanced at the clock, the hour hand resting on the two. 'An angel. That's what you are.' Though she would pack lunch tomorrow to make sure she had something. She hadn't realised how hard it could be to get away from the ward to the cafeteria. She'd expected that on night duty but not through the day.

Myra tilted her head to scrutinise her. 'Have you had time to stop for a few minutes?'

Trina sat back and gestured to the chair beside her. 'Not yet. But I do now. And I will.' She took the china mug Myra carried and took a sip before she put it down on the desk beside her. 'Ah!' She smiled at the older lady. 'I seriously needed that.' She looked at the mug again and picked it up. Took another sip and closed her eyes. 'The world won't stop turning if I don't achieve everything today.'

Myra laughed. 'Something I've learnt since I came here. So how is it going? Is it strange to be on the ward in the daytime?'

Trina glanced around the sunlit reception area. The windows that showed the gardens. The sunlight slanting across the polished wooden floors. 'It is. And there are so many people I need to talk to.' She pretended to shudder. 'Business requirements have given me interaction overload. Present company excluded, of course.'

'I won't be offended.' Myra looked at her with concern. 'Are you sure you wouldn't prefer sitting in the tea room and I could answer the phone for you while you finish your tart?'

Trina laughed. 'No. This is a social conversation. Much more fun. Besides, I haven't seen you for days. How are you? How is married life? Any adventurous plans?'

'I'm well. Ridiculously content, and I'm trying to talk Reg into coming away with me on a cruising holiday. There's a last-minute deal that's breaking my heart not to take.'

Trina could see Myra at a Captain's Cocktail Party, dressed to the nines in those stunning vintage outfits she seemed to source at will. Trina could never find anything when she looked in the pre-loved section. Or if she did she looked ridiculous. But Myra looked soft and elegant and stunningly stylish. She sighed and let the envy go. She hadn't really thought much of clothes since Ed. 'That sounds fun. Does he like the idea?'

'More than I thought he would. But it all depends if he finds locum relief for the practice. I'm a little keen for him to scale right back but he's become immersed in the bay and the hospital.'

Trina could see why Myra wanted to play. 'I haven't seen him out on his surfboard lately.'

'He still goes out every Sunday with his son. It's lovely to see. Says he doesn't have the need to get out of bed at the crack of dawn now—especially with me in it.' Myra smiled with just a hint of pink in her cheeks and Trina smiled back.

'Understandable.' She thought of Finn. Her own cheeks heated and she dipped her head and took a sip from her mug to hide it. Of course he was the locum Myra hoped for, and of course she wasn't blushing just because of Myra's mention of mornings in bed. 'Is he hopeful of the locum situation?'

Myra sighed. 'There's a young doctor in town he's had a chat with. Some family issue that's keeping him from starting, but hopefully that will sort soon. If not, I think he should advertise.'

'I met the one I think he's talking about. Finlay Foley. He's a single dad. Has a delightful little one-year-old.'

Myra unwrapped the tart from its white paper bag and pushed it towards Trina. 'That's the one. That's right—Reg said he had a daughter. What's he like?'

'He's an amazing dad. Anyone can see that. It's a wonder you haven't seen him walking along the beach with his little girl on his back.'

Myra's eyes brightened. She lifted her head in delight and glanced towards the general direction of the beach way below, though she wouldn't be able to see it. 'Oh. I have seen him. Younger than I expected. I didn't think of him as a doctor. Looks too young.' She lowered her voice and said suggestively, 'And handsome.'

Trina laughed. 'I used to see them in the mornings after work when I walked. Been here for a month but I've only really talked to him this weekend.' Funny how it felt as if she'd known Finn for ages. What was that? 'His little girl turned one yesterday. And I did mention Marni as a suggestion for childminding. He's thinking about it.'

'Oh, that's marvellous news. And a really good idea. Marni is the perfect mother to those tiny boys. I might get Reg to give him a nudge—not a big nudger is my Reg. But I would like to catch that sailing if possible.'

Trina laughed. 'You might have a surprise when you get home, then.' She picked up the tart and bit into the buttery pastry with slow enjoyment. The tang of Parmesan cheese, fresh spring onions and cream made her eyes roll. She took another bite and savoured. Before she knew, the tart was gone. 'Goodness, Myra. I should have a standing order for those.'

Myra laughed. 'My man is a bit pleased with my cooking.'

Trina picked up her coffee and then paused as a thought intruded. If Finn took over Dr Southwell's practice while he was away, he'd be working in the hospital. And he'd probably walk through Maternity. Might even seek her out as a friendly face. Not that everyone wasn't friendly at Lighthouse Bay. Maybe he'd even come over if they needed a third for a tricky birth. Their own personal paediatrician.

Her belly seemed to warm and it had nothing to do with food and hot coffee, though they had been good. She finished the last of the coffee not quite in the present moment. It was all positive because he was a paediatrician. Good for those babies that didn't breathe as well as you expected them to. *Oh, my.*

'You look much better for stopping and eating,' Myra said with some satisfaction. She stood up. 'I won't bother you any longer and let you get on before your afternoon midwives come on.'

'You're never a bother. More of a life-saver. Thank you.' She glanced down at the empty crumpled white bag. 'You've made my day.' In more ways than one.

Trina finished work at five-thirty that evening and decided to walk quickly down the breakwall and blow the stress of the day away. The administration side of the maternity unit would take a little time to get used to but she'd mastered most of the things that had slowed her up. The joy of finishing work and not having to worry about sleep until it was dark felt like a sweet novelty. Especially when, on her way back, she saw that Finn and Piper, wrapped in scarves, were walking too. Finn swung along effortlessly, the bundle on his back wriggling when she saw Catrina.

Finn raised his hand and changed direction and she sat on the breakwall and waited for him to reach her. As they approached she couldn't help watching his stride as his strong thighs closed the distance between them. His broad shoulders were silhouetted against the ocean and his eyes crinkled with delight as he came up to her.

The smile he gave her made the waiting

even more worth it. She realised she'd been staring and spoke first. 'Hello. How did Piper go today?'

He patted Piper's leg. 'She didn't want to leave when I went to pick her up.'

Trina tried to hide her smile behind a sympathetic look but it didn't stick.

He pretended to scowl at her. 'You think that's amusing?'

She straightened her face. 'I'm pretty sure you were relieved too.'

He dropped his mock-injured façade. 'Absolutely. It felt good to see her so comfortable in another setting. And I owe that to you.' A genuine heartfelt smile which she might just snapshot and pull out later when she got home. 'Thank you, Catrina.'

She'd done nothing. He seemed so serious. And he seemed to expect some comment. 'For the little I did you're very welcome, Finn.'

'I'm serious.' Had he read her mind? 'In fact, Piper and I would like to invite you to our house to share dinner on Thursday night. In celebration of her finding childcare and me starting work next Monday. If you don't have a previous engagement?' There was a tiny hesitation at the last comment and she wondered why he thought she would.

'No previous engagement.'

Was that relief on his face? 'Just our usual slap-up meal. So you don't have to cook when you get home.' He hurried on. 'It will be early and if you needed to you could still be home by dark.'

She laughed. It would certainly be an early dinner as night fell about seven. 'I finish at five-thirty so can be there by six. Though sometimes the wheels fall off at work and that could slow me down or make me cancel.'

He shrugged. 'Been there. We'll take that as we have to.'

Trina smiled. Of course. A paed would know that. 'In that case, lovely. Thank you.' She tweaked the baby toes at Finn's chest. 'Thank you for the invitation, Piper.' The little girl gurgled and said, 'Mum, Mum, Mum.'

Trina pretended she didn't see Finn's wince. 'I bet she was saying that all the time at Marni's house. The boys will come ahead on their speaking with her there.'

He still looked subdued so she went on. 'Soon they'll be able to say *fiss*.'

Finn seemed to shake himself. She saw him

cast his mind back and his smile grew. Could see when he remembered the rock pool. Saw the relief for the change of focus.

His smile dipped to rueful. 'You're right.' Then he straightened and gave her his full attention again. 'How was your first day as the boss?'

'Administrative. Hats off to Ellie for never complaining about all the paperwork and ordering. But it's well worth it to have finished work at this time and still get a full night's sleep. It will be amazing when Daylight Saving comes back in and it doesn't get dark till after eight at night.'

CHAPTER ELEVEN

Finn

FINN SHIFTED ON the hard boardwalk, listened, but inside he thought, *Yes, she's coming on Thursday.* He felt like dancing a jig. Didn't want to think about why. The tension that had been building slowly released. She made him feel like a teenager which, though disconcerting, made a good change from feeling like an old man most of the time.

He'd considered the invitation from every angle because it had become increasingly important he didn't scare Catrina away and he still remembered her warnings when they'd first met. Enjoying her company had lifted his life from survival to anticipation. And he anticipated that Catrina could be great company for the foreseeable future if he stayed careful.

But she'd said she didn't want a relationship. It suited him fine, he kept telling himself that, and it had nothing to do with the fact that every time he saw her he noticed something new about her.

Like that especially golden strand of hair that fell across her forehead and made him want to move it out of her eyes. Or the way the soft skin on the curve of her long neck made him want to stroke that vulnerable spot with one finger. Just to assess if it felt like the velvet it resembled.

Of course it was all about Piper—she needed to have a female figure in her life who didn't demand anything—but Catrina gave so much warmth he could feel himself thawing more each day. Or maybe it was the fact he'd told himself he'd change now that Piper's first birthday had passed.

He tamped down the suspicion it could be selfish to blow so persistently on the flame of their friendship when he didn't have much to offer, was still married in fact, but he could feel the restoration of his soul and sensibilities. And the better he was in himself the better he was for Piper.

So he'd considered all the barriers she might have had to agreeing to a first dinner date and had methodically worked on arranging for them to disappear. To make it easy for both of them.

It would be a celebration—Piper's care with Marni and his new job.

She started work early the first four days of the week—so he'd invited her on Thursday—she had to eat, so no reason not to grab a free meal from him on the way home.

Plus he was hoping to set up some connections with her over the coming weekend and that would seem more impromptu if he mentioned those on Thursday.

And the big card—Catrina had to be curious to see his house. It had all paid off.

'Did you like the Southwells' surgery?' Her voice startled him back into the present moment. He thought back to earlier in the day. To the white cottage that held Dr Southwell's medical rooms.

'It's quaint. Not as strange as it could have been. A small practice, one receptionist, and I'd have my own room to settle into, which is always better than using someone else's. I'll have all my equipment sent ASAP.' Or he could drive back and get it, but the idea made him shudder.

Catrina's voice grounded him. 'That's good. Did you see any patients?'

'You mean behave like a real doctor?' He smiled at her. 'Not yet. But I will start with those with urgent needs and Reg seems to think I could concentrate on children, which would suit me very well, and meet a need for the community.'

Catrina nodded slowly as she thought about it. 'I know at the base hospital it takes a few weeks for the paediatrician to see new patients. Perhaps you would even have some of those mums driving their children over this way, like the Lighthouse Bay mums go to the base for the service. Certainly easier for people like Marni to take the boys for their premmie check-ups.'

'Plus I'd be available for general patients when it was busy, but it seemed pretty sleepy today. Perfect hours of work for a dad with a little girl to consider.'

'Did he talk about you covering the general patients in the hospital when he goes away?'

'He did say that. Which is fine with me. It's not a big hospital and I can read up on who's in there when the time comes.'

Catrina stifled a laugh and he glanced at

her. 'Dr Southwell's wife is keen on a cruise that leaves soon. Don't be surprised if it happens faster than you think.'

He raised his brows in question. 'Inside information?'

'I saw Myra today and she did mention she hoped Reg would find someone soon and that she had a boat she didn't want to miss.'

'Thanks for the heads-up. I'm sure I'd manage. That's what locums do, after all.' But everything seemed to be happening very fast. 'Do they get called out at night much?'

'Rarely. And it's shared call. So no more than three nights a week as a twenty-four-hour cover.' He watched her expression change as she realised that leaving Piper could be a problem on those nights.

'Hmm.' He could tell they were both thinking of Marni's flexibility as a day care mum.

'Something to think about,' Catrina said with massive understatement. 'And it won't be a problem unless Dr Southwell takes Myra away.'

'Which apparently might be sooner rather than later.' Had he started work too soon? Would his boss have an idea? Was it too much to ask the babysitter for Piper to sleep over those nights? As long as he didn't go over the forty hours, maybe it would be okay? His feeling that everything had fallen into place shifted again and he sighed. He wondered, not for the first time, how single parents managed to work at all.

Thursday arrived and Finn had been cooking, creating and carving in the kitchen. Something his mother had tried to instil in his sister but she'd found more fertile ground with Finn. He'd loved the times he and his mother had spent cooking, and in his short marriage the kitchen had been his domain at the weekend. It felt good to make something apart from nutritious finger food for Piper.

So, tonight a roast dinner. Something his wife had scoffed at but something he loved and missed—possibly because when they'd called at Marni's house the smell had reminded him how much he'd enjoyed a roast dinner as a child. And when Catrina had shared their lunch that first weekend they'd started talking—was it only a week ago?—she'd chosen a roast beef sandwich so she must like meat.

He'd slow roasted the beef and it lay, carved

and foil-covered, in the oven with a veggie dish of potatoes, sweet potato, pumpkin and whole small onions. A side of fresh beans, carrots and broccoli would have Piper in seventh heaven. His jug of gravy was reheating and fresh bread rolls were on the table with real butter waiting.

He glanced around. The house remained a little spartan in his areas and cluttered in Piper's. She lay on her side in the playpen talking to her bunny. She'd had her bath and was dressed in her pyjamas, now looking a little sleepy, and he wondered if he should give her dinner early in case Catrina was late.

But it would be hard to dish up Piper's and not pick for himself. His belly rumbled. Just then a knock sounded on the door and he put the oven mitt back on the bench. He felt an unaccustomed eagerness as he crossed the room and tried to damp it down. They were just friends.

Then he opened the door and there she stood, the afternoon sunlight a glow around her and an almost shy smile on her beautiful lips. Her eyes were clear and bright and her lovely dark auburn hair swung loose in the sea breeze with glints of gold dancing like ribbons.

She'd changed out of her work clothes. Stood calmly clad in a pretty sundress and a cream cardigan, her bare legs brown and long with painted toes peeping out of coral-coloured sandals. Finn admonished himself not to feel too special because she'd taken the time to change for him.

He couldn't believe how good she looked. Needed to remind himself he barely knew this woman, but it was as if he'd been waiting a long time for this moment. Found himself saying softly, 'You truly are a picture.'

Catrina blushed but lifted her head. He liked the way she did that. No false modesty that she hadn't put in any effort. 'Thank you.' She lifted her chin higher and sniffed slowly. 'And you have a divine aroma floating out of your house.'

He laughed. 'I'll be glad when we can eat. It's been teasing me for hours now.' Not the only sensation that had been teasing him but he was trying not to think about Catrina's mouth.

She laughed then, her lips curving entic-ingly, but, unlike another woman, this one held no expectations to use her beauty and the tension stayed behind in the swirl of salt and sunshine outside as he invited her in and shut the door.

CHAPTER TWELVE

Trina

TRINA STEPPED INTO Finn's house, still feeling a little mentally fragile at the tiny handprints she'd seen on the step. There was something so heart-wrenchingly adorable about a dad doing cement prints with his baby daughter. If she wasn't careful she'd end up falling for this guy so hard she'd be vulnerable again to loss.

It was a sobering thought.

Then, to make matters more serious, when Finn had opened the door her heart had lifted at the sight of him. Two steps up, he'd towered over her, but his quick movement sideways as if he couldn't wait for her to come in had softened the impression of feeling small into a feeling of being very much appreciated.

She couldn't miss the approval and delight

on his face as his gaze had run over her. So, yes, she was glad she'd spent the extra fifteen minutes changing and refreshing her make-up. Brushing her hair loose—not something she did often but it did feel freeing, and apparently it met with Finn's approval.

She felt the warmth of his body as she squeezed past him into the bright and airy room, and more warmth when she saw the way Piper pulled herself up and smiled at her. She bent down and blew a kiss at the little girl, who clutched her bunny and smiled back. Then to be enveloped in the warmth of expectation with a table set and meal prepared for her—well, it did seem a little too good to be true.

She turned back to look at Finn—Dr Finn—lounging against the closed door as if savouring the sight of her. His strong arms were crossed against his chest as if taking the time to watch her reaction. She was getting a little heady here. She licked unexpectedly dry lips. 'I'm feeling special.'

'Good. You are special. Piper and I can thank you for the help you've given us.'

She hadn't done much. But her grandmother had said, *Always answer a compli-*

ment with gratitude and don't correct the giver. 'Thank you.' But she could change the subject. 'It looks great in here. So light and airy and fresh. I love the wood grain in the floor.'

He crossed said floorboards towards her and pulled out her chair. 'Silky oak. It was under the carpet. Feels nice underfoot and I can hear Piper coming up behind me when I'm not looking. Though I had a polisher come and help me rub it back and polish it by hand. Hardest day's work I'd done all year.' He grinned at her and she could see he'd enjoyed the challenge.

'And what did Miss Piper do while you were playing around on the floor?'

'Luckily it was a typical Lighthouse Bay day—sunny—and we put up a little pergola. She stayed just outside the door in her playpen and kept us hard at it.'

Lucky her. To watch two men rubbing polish into wood for a few hours. Something very nice about that thought, Trina mused as she took the seat he held out for her.

Finn crossed to pick up Piper and poked her toes into her high chair and she snaked her way in like a little otter. Then he clipped a pink rubber bib around her neck. Piper did look excited at the thought of food.

'Can I help?' Trina asked, feeling a tad useless.

'It's a tiny kitchen nook, so you girls sit here while I produce my masterpiece and wait on you.' Then he glanced at his fidgety daughter. 'But you could hand Piper that crust on the plastic plate. She can chew on that while she waits for her veggies to cool.' He cast a sideways glance at Trina. 'I learnt it's better to give her something to chew on when she's in the chair or she starts to climb around when I'm not looking.'

'Ah—' Trina hurriedly passed the crust to Piper '—there you go, madam. Diversion tactics.'

Piper held out her hand and gleefully accepted the morsel and Finn strode the few steps to the kitchen bench and back across with the first plate and a jug of gravy.

'Roast veggies. Gravy.' He deposited his load and spun away, then was back in moments with a heaped plate of carved roast beef, the barest hint of pink at the centre of each slice. 'If you don't like it rare the more well-done pieces are at the edge.'

Trina's mouth had begun watering as the food began to arrive. 'I think I'm in heaven. It was busy today and I missed lunch. Plus I haven't had a roast for two years.' Not since before Ed's illness. Guilt and regret swamped her and she tried to keep it from her face.

Finn took a swift glance at her and said smoothly, 'It's all Marni's fault. That first day we visited. The way her house smelled of roast dinner did me in.' She decided he was very determined that they would enjoy the meal. Good thing too.

Trina pulled herself together and asked, 'So is this Piper's first roast dinner?'

'Indeed. More cause for celebration.' He leaned and poured them both a glass of cold water from the carafe on the table. The water glasses looked like crystal to Trina. 'Let's drink to that.' Then he raised his hand to hers and they touched glasses with a tell-tale perfect *ching* and her melancholy fell away as they sipped. Life was pretty darn good.

He indicated the food. 'You serve yours and I'll fix Piper.' Finn dished some veggies and meat onto Piper's cartoon-illustrated plastic plate and swiftly cut them into bite-sized pieces.

This was all done so efficiently that Trina found herself smiling. Such a maternal thing to do but this dad had it covered.

She arranged her own plate, finishing with a generous serve of gravy, and sat back to wait for Finn.

He wasn't far behind. He topped his meal off with his gravy and then looked up to meet her eyes. *'Bon appétit.'*

They didn't talk much as they ate, neither did they rush, and Trina glanced around as she savoured the subtle and not so subtle flavours of a well-cooked roast dinner. Marvelled at the decorating touches that showed this man's love for his daughter. A mobile of seashells over the cot, a run of circus animals in a wallpaper panel behind her bed. An alphabet mat on the floor with a Piper-sized chair on it. A row of small dolls in bright dresses.

She indicated the dolls with her fork. 'So these are the ladies you talk to?'

'All the time. Especially the brunette on the end. Remarkable conversationalist, really.'

'I can imagine.' She smiled at the dark-haired doll which, at a stretch, could look a little like Trina herself.

'Do you like our home?' Needy? Keen for her approval? But there was something endearing about that.

She nodded sagely. 'I think Piper will be a famous decorator one day.'

She was teasing him but it must have been the right thing to say because his pleasure was almost palpable. 'Remind me to show you the shower. We have very nice tiles.'

'I'll make sure I do that.' And she allowed herself to consider the possibility of a future here. With this man and his daughter. At the very least as friends and with a potential for more…but she wouldn't rush. Couldn't rush. And neither could he.

The thought crashed in. Who knew where his wife was? The thought brought a deluge of dampness to her sunny spirits and she looked down at her food, which suddenly didn't taste as good as it had.

'So tell me about the rest of your week. Did Piper still want to stay at Marni's when you went to pick her up after a full day or did she miss you?'

'Both. Marni is wonderful with her. And your Myra has booked her drop-and-go cruise. A five-nighter to Tasmania. They leave Sunday. So call and three-day rosters at the hospital. Piper will have to stay over when I'm on call. Though they've managed to give me only the one night call, which I appreciate.'

'Wow. You've dived into work with a vengeance.'

'I should have done it earlier. I'm feeling more connected to humanity every day.' He glanced up at her with definite warmth. 'Though that could have been you.'

Glad he thought she was human. But that wasn't what he meant and she knew it. Her face heated and she looked down at her almost empty plate. 'Thank you, kind sir.' She lifted her head and shook the hair away from her face. It was getting hot in here. 'One night seems like the perfect answer. That's not too bad as a start. When did you say that night was?'

'Next Thursday. We'll see how she goes. Marni's not worried.'

She could have offered for a Thursday night but she was glad he hadn't asked. She wasn't ready for that much commitment. 'Well, good luck.' She lifted her glass of water. 'And here's to your first week at the hospital. I'll look forward to your smiling face.'

'I'll try to remember to smile.'

CHAPTER THIRTEEN

Finn

BY MONDAY MORNING, his first day in the hospital, Catrina continued to seep into Finn's thoughts with alarming regularity and he was feeling just as strange about that as he was about the new work model he'd slipped into. A general GP, admittedly with extra specialist paediatric consults on the side, and a rural hospital generalist as well. With maternity cover? Never thought he'd see the day.

Over the weekend he and Catrina had met a lot, each meeting better than the last, plus they'd talked about the hospital and the patients he'd probably find come Monday. About how the medical input had changed since the new midwifery model had started, even some of the times that Dr Southwell had been called away from the main hospital to provide back-up in Maternity.

He could see Catrina enjoyed their discussions and, to be truthful, he was a little curious to see how it all worked. They'd bumped into each other often. Intentionally on his part and, he suspected glumly, unintentionally on hers.

He'd managed the Friday morning beach bump into when, after his own walk, he'd offered to share the breakwall with Catrina, Piper on his back, and they'd spent more than an hour together talking non-stop.

Saturday morning, after Catrina's scuba lesson, he and Piper had been back in their rock pool at just the right time for her to walk past them again and fortuitously share an early lunch as Catrina offered to return last week's lunch shout at the beach café.

Saturday night he and Piper had been invited to a barbecue dinner at Ellie and Sam's and, of course, Catrina had been there as she lived next door.

Naturally he'd spoken to other people but they'd spent most of the time standing together. He'd had an excellent conversation with Sam on the strangeness of working in a cottage hospital after coming from a tertiary health facility and Myra had shaken his hand and thanked him for making it possible to drag her husband away on a cruise. But the stand-out moments were those watching Catrina's quiet rapport with the other dinner guests.

His eyes had drifted in her direction way too often.

The best had been on Sunday when Catrina had asked if Piper—and Finn—could come and help her choose colours for her new carpet and cushions and they'd had a hilarious day at the nearest large town choosing colours via a one-year-old in a stroller.

A huge weekend, in fact, but one that had passed without kissing her once. And that also was something he couldn't get out of his mind.

Her mouth. So mobile, always smiling and doing that soft chortling thing when he said something to amuse her—a new skill he seemed to have acquired that did more to heal his soul than anything else.

Or that unconscious, but luscious, lip-pursing she did when she seriously considered something he said. Or just her mouth looking downright kissable when he didn't expect it, and he was having a hard time not drifting off and staring at the lift of a corner or the flash of white teeth.

He didn't remember being this fixated on Piper's mother when he'd met her. There had certainly been attraction, almost a forest fire of heat and lust culminating in a headlong rush into marriage when their contraception had failed. More his idea than hers and he had certainly paid the price for that.

But he was coming to the conclusion that he must have been meant to be Piper's daddy because he couldn't imagine life without his baby girl so he thanked Clancy for that. There was a bit of healing in there somewhere and he wasn't sure he didn't owe Catrina for that thought too.

But Catrina? Well? He needed to slow down and not lose the plot, but Catrina made him want to be better at being himself, a better person, even a better partner since he'd obviously fallen short on that last time.

His attraction to Catrina had been exquisitely stoked by want and need, and he feared—or was that dared to hope?—she might be coming to care for him too.

This morning, as he climbed the hill to the little white hospital sitting on a cliff, he hoped that very much. He glanced at the cottage garden as he approached for his first day as visiting medical officer and could feel his spirits soar as he strode towards a new perspective of Catrina at work.

The ocean glittered a sapphire blue today, brighter and more jewel-like than he could remember seeing. Piper had been as lively as a grig being handed over to Marni and the boys. And he, well, he was back at work, feeling almost comfortable already in Reg's practice, like a normal human being. It had taken a year of shadow. And a week. And Catrina.

Except for the colour of the ocean, Catrina had a lot to do with most of his forward progress. Though maybe all the colours were appearing brighter this week because of her as well.

Reg had suggested he call into Maternity first—'Around eight, my boy!'—to see if any women were in labour—'Just so you can be aware.' And then attend to his hospital round on the other side of the small white building.

He suspected that the midwives didn't need the visit but Reg clearly felt paternal in his concern for them. Finn thought it prudent not to share that insight with Catrina.

But what a gift of an excuse, he thought as he stepped through the automatic front door to Maternity and glanced around for her.

Instead, a nurse he'd met on his orientation round with Reg on Friday came in through the side door from the main hospital at a run and her relief at seeing him alerted his instincts faster than her voice. 'Dr Foley—please follow me through to the birthing suite. Urgently!'

The smile slipped from Finn's face and he nodded and followed.

When he entered, he saw Catrina standing over a neonatal resuscitation trolley, her fingers encircling the little chest with her thumb pressing cardiac massage over the baby's sternum in a rhythmic count.

Another nurse held the tiny face mask over the baby's face, inflating the chest with intermittent positive pressure ventilations after every third compression.

Finn stopped beside them, glanced at the seconds ticking past on the trolley clock that indicated time since birth. It showed ninety seconds.

Catrina looked up and the concentrated expression on her face faltered for the briefest moment and he saw the concern and the relief on her face. Then she looked at the clock as well. Her voice remained calm but crisp.

'Rhiannon's baby was born two minutes ago, short cord snapped during delivery so probable neonatal blood loss. Baby is just not getting the hang of this breathing business.' Her voice came out remarkably steady and he filed that away to tell her later.

'Heart rate less than sixty for the last thirty seconds so we added cardiac compression to the IPPV and it's just come back to eighty.' She loosened her fingers around the baby's chest and turned down the oxygen to keep the levels similar to where a two-minute-old baby would normally be. Too much oxygen held as many risks as not enough oxygen for babies.

'This is the paediatrician, Dr Foley, Rhiannon,' she called across to the mum, who was holding the hand of an older woman, concern etched on their faces.

Finn lifted his hand and smiled reassuringly. Because the fact the baby had picked up his heartbeat was an excellent sign. 'Give us a few minutes and I'll come across and explain.'

He glanced at the pulse oximeter someone had strapped to the flaccid pale wrist. 'You're keeping the oxygen levels perfect. Umbilical catheter then,' Finn said calmly. 'I'll top up the fluids and the rest should stabilise.'

'The set-up is in the second drawer. There's a diagram on the lid because we don't use it often.'

He retrieved the transparent plastic box and put it on the nearby bench, squirted antiseptic on his hands and began to assemble the intravenous line that would be inserted a little way into the baby's umbilical cord stump and give a ready-made large bore venous entry point to replace the fluids lost.

He glanced at Catrina. 'Warmed fluids?'

'Cupboard outside the door.' The nurse he'd arrived with handed Catrina the clipboard she'd taken to jot observations on and slipped out to get the fluids. By the time he had all the syringes and tubing set she was back and they primed the line with the warmed fluids and set it aside.

Finn squirted the antiseptic on his hands again and donned the sterile gloves to wipe the baby's belly around the cord with an antiseptic swab, and wiped the cord stump liberally with the solution.

After placing a towel on the baby's belly to give himself a sterile field he could work from, he tied the soft sterile tape around the base of the finger-thick umbilical cord. The tape was a safety measure, so that when they removed the cord clamp Catrina had fastened at birth, he could pull the tape tight around the umbilical cord to control any further blood loss.

Once the tape was in place and fastened firmly, Catrina looked at Finn, who smiled reassuringly because he doubted it was something she did on a newly cut cord very often, and watched her remove the cord clamp with only a trace of anxiety.

Finn nodded to himself, satisfied—no bleeding—then sliced off the nerveless ragged edge of the snapped cord closer to the baby's belly with a scalpel blade, the white tape preventing any further blood loss. Now he could easily see the vessels inside where he wanted to put the tubing.

Using fine artery forceps, he captured one

edge of the cord and then offered the forceps to Catrina to hold to free up his other hand.

With the cord now pulled upright, Finn lifted the catheter and another pair of forceps to insert the end into the gaping vessel of the vein in the umbilical cord. He glimpsed the nurse from the main hospital looking wide-eyed and said quietly, 'It's easy to tell which is the vein, being the largest and softest vessel of the three in the cord. That's the one that leads to the heart.'

Catrina asked, 'Do you have to turn the catheter to insert it? Aren't the vessels spiral?'

'Yes, spiral so when the cord is pulled in utero there's give and spring, the longer the cut cord the more spiral you have to traverse until you get to the bloodstream. That's why I cut this fairly short. Not too short that you don't leave yourself a back-up plan, though.'

The fine clear intravenous tubing disappeared just below the baby's abdominal skin. A sudden swirl of blood mixed with the warmed fluid Finn had primed the tubing with.

'And we're in,' Finn said with satisfaction. He adjusted the three-way tap on the line with one hand and slowly injected the warmed saline fluid with a fat syringe into the baby's bloodstream. 'Ten mils per kilo will do it, and I'd say this little tyke is about three kilos.'

He glanced at Catrina, who watched the monitor to see the baby's heart rate slowly increasing. She nodded. He then glanced at her colleague, still calmly applying intermittent puffs of air into the baby's lungs, and then watched as the tiny flaccid hand slowly clenched as tone returned to the baby's body and he began to flex and twitch.

Finn looked over at the mum. 'Not long now.'

'Get ready to tighten the cord again, Catrina,' he said softly and, once the full amount of fluid had been injected and Catrina was ready, he turned the tap on the infusion and removed the syringe.

'We'll just wait a few minutes before we remove it in case we need to give any drugs, but I think that will do the trick.'

CHAPTER FOURTEEN

Trina

TRINA'S GALLOPING PULSE slowed as the baby's heart rate began to rise above eighty. Her hand loosened on the resuscitation trolley she seemed to have gripped as Finn did his thing. After what had seemed like forever the baby's heart rate hit a hundred and ten and finally the baby blinked and struggled, grimaced against the mask and, in the most beautiful screech in the world, he began to cry. The tension in the room fluttered and fell like a diving bird and she watched Finn slowly withdraw the tubing from the vein. She tightened the cord as it came clear and then snapped on a new umbilical clamp close to the end of the stump. Done.

Baby threw his hands and kicked his feet and they pushed the resuscitation trolley closer to the mum's bed so he could be handed across with the pulse oximeter still strapped to his wrist.

Trina considered removing it as he'd become so vigorous with the replacement of fluid but it would be easier to monitor instead of listening with a stethoscope so, despite the tangle of wires, she left him connected and pressed his bare skin to his mother's naked breasts.

Once baby was settled on his mother, his breathing clear and unobstructed, she could relax a little more. A blanket covered them both, and she glanced at Finn, standing at the side of the trolley, his beautiful mouth soft as he watched the baby and mother finally together. His eyes shone with pleasure and he gave a little nod just before he saw Trina looking at him.

The smile he gave her, one of warmth and pride and appreciation, made her clutch her throat and heat surged into her cheeks. She'd done nothing.

When she looked back at him he was watching the mum again, his eyes still soft as he spoke to her.

'Hello there. Congratulations. As Trina

said, I'm Dr Foley, the paediatrician, and your little boy looks great now. Snapped cords are fairly rare, but if a baby grows in utero with a short umbilical cord…' he smiled that warm and reassuring smile that seemed to seep right down to the soles of Trina's feet and he wasn't even looking at her '…which he is perfectly entitled to do.' He shrugged. 'Not surprisingly, though it *is* always a surprise, they can run out of stretch at birth and the cord can pull too tight.'

Rhiannon nodded and her own mother sat back with relief to see her grandchild safely snuggled into Rhiannon's arms.

Finn went on. 'Babies don't have a lot of blood to spare so some extra fluid through that intravenous line allowed his heart to get back into the faster rhythm it needs. As you saw, it's usually a fairly dramatic improvement. We'll do some blood tests and if we need to we'll talk about a blood transfusion. But he looks good.'

'Too much drama for me,' Rhiannon said, as she cuddled her baby close to her chest. Trina could agree with that. Now that she had time to think about it, she had to admit that Finn's appearance had been a miracle she'd very much needed. But there wasn't time for that yet as she began to attend to all the things that needed doing in the immediate time after a baby had been born.

Two and a half hours later Trina had settled Rhiannon and baby Jackson into their room, and the myriad of paperwork, forms and data entry had been sorted. The nurse from the hospital had stayed to help Trina tidy the ward because Faith, the midwife from night duty, had already stayed later than normal. Trina glanced at the clock, just ten-thirty, so, on top of the tasks still waiting to be done, she did need a moment to sit back in the chair and consider the excitement of the morning.

It had been a little too exciting but thankfully Finn had appeared at exactly the right moment without needing to be called. An opportune thing.

Like he did at that moment. Striding through the doors from the main hospital as if he owned the place.

She felt a smile stretch her face. 'I was just thinking about you.'

His laughing eyes made her belly flip-flop and caution flooded her. He had a wife. Somewhere.

'Good things, I hope?' he said.

She shook her head. Pretended to think about it. 'How I didn't need you this morning and you just pushed in.' Teasing him.

His face froze for a second and she slid her hand over her mouth in horror, saying quickly, 'Joke. A very mean joke. Especially when you were so good. I'm sorry.' But she could feel the creases in her cheeks as she smiled because his shock had been palpable when the statement had been totally ridiculous. He must have known she'd needed him desperately. She had no idea why she'd said such a crazy thing except to startle him. Or maybe because she'd been trying to hide how absolutely thrilled she was that he'd come back to see her when she'd thought he would have been long gone from the hospital.

This man brought out very strange urges in her. At least she wasn't giggling like a twit. She was saying bizarre things instead.

He laughed a little sheepishly. 'I was worried for a minute there.'

She looked up at him. Seriously? 'Don't be. Sorry. I was never so glad to see anybody in my life. My pulse was about a hundred and sixty.' And it wasn't far from that now with him standing so close, which would not do.

He studied her. That didn't help the galloping heart rate. 'Well, you looked as cool as a cucumber.'

'On the outside. Good to know.' Hopefully she looked that way now as well—especially with her brain telling her to do stupid things in fight and flight mode. 'But, seriously, you were very slick with inserting that umbi line. Most impressive.'

And she had no doubt her eyes were telling him a tad more than she was saying because he smiled back at her with a lot more warmth than she deserved after what she'd just done to him. He sat down beside her at the desk.

To hide the heat in her cheeks she looked past his shoulder towards Rhiannon's room and murmured, 'It would have been very tense to keep resuscitating a baby who didn't improve as we expected. He really needed that fluid in his system to get him circulating properly.'

He didn't say anything so she looked at him. He was studying her intently again and her face grew hotter. 'What?'

'We were lucky. That was all it was. I'm wondering if you could call me for the next couple of births through the day while Piper is in care, just so I can sneak in a refresher course on normal birth. It's a long time since my term in Obstetrics working towards my OB Diploma and I want to be up to speed if an emergency occurs.'

His diffidence surprised her. 'Of course, you're welcome. I call in a nurse from the hospital as my second but I can easily call you instead if we have time. Or as well. I don't mind. And I can run a simulation through the latest changes in post-partum haemorrhage and prem labour if you like.'

'Excellent. I've been doing some reading but things aren't always the same when you get to the different hospital sites.'

'We're a birth centre not a hospital, even though we're joined by an external corridor. So all of our women are low risk.' But things still happened. Not with the regularity you saw in a major hospital but they did deal with first line emergencies until a woman or her baby could be transferred to higher care.

He nodded. 'Is that your first snapped cord?'

'My first here.' She shook her head, still

a little shocked. 'We've had them tear and bleed but to actually just break like that was a shock.'

'It's rare. Had probably torn already and when the last stretch happened at birth it broke—but you handled it well, getting the clamp on so quickly. I've seen some much worse situations.'

'I kept expecting him to get better, like nearly all babies do when you give them a puff or two, but by the time you arrived I was getting worried.'

He nodded. 'Hypovolemia will do that. How's Mum?'

'Taken it in her stride. Said her angels were looking after her and baby Jackson.' She thought he'd laugh.

'Useful things, angels.' Then, in an aside, 'My mother was a medium. I should have listened to her.'

He shrugged and Trina tried not to gape. His turn to say something off the wall, maybe, or he could be pulling her leg because he grinned at her surprise.

He changed the subject before she could ask. 'Today Jackson also had the midwives and doctor.' He grinned. 'Shall I go down and see if she has any more questions now she's had a chance to think about it?'

Trina stood up as well. Off balance by his throwaway comment about his mother... and his proximity. Moving to a new location sounded like a great idea, she thought, still mentally shaking her head to clear it. That had been the last thing she'd expected him to say. But she'd ask more later. This moment, here at work, wasn't the time. Angel medium? Seriously, she was dying to find out.

'Great idea. Thank you.' She stood up and followed him. Finn was thoughtful, kind and darn slick as a paediatrician. Lighthouse Bay might just have to count its blessings to have another fabulous doctor in the wings when they needed him. Speaking of wings... Angels? Her head spun as she followed him down the hallway.

Over the next four days while Finn covered the hospital, he shared three births with Trina between breakfast and morning tea. It was almost as if the mothers were on a timetable of morning births to make it easy for him to be able to watch and even catch one.

She could tell he was enjoying himself.

Basking in the magic that was birth. But the busyness meant she didn't get a chance to ask about him. About his mother's angels. About his childhood. About his marriage—not that she would! The woman who had given birth to Piper and what had happened to her.

Trina hoped they were at the stage of friendship where she could ask about at least some of those things soon. But then again, she hadn't shared anything of her past either. Maybe they should just leave it all in the past and keep talking about Lighthouse Bay nineteen to the dozen like they had been. Share the past slowly because she was probably reading too much into his interest.

Lighthouse Bay Maternity must have decided to draw in the babies for Dr Finn, because they just kept coming. The overdue ones arrived, the early ones came early, and the more time they spent together with new babies and new families the more her curiosity about Finn's world before he came here grew.

He left soon after each birth to continue his appointments at the surgery but returned at late lunchtime with his sandwiches to talk about the morning's events.

On Thursday, his last hospital shift before Dr Southwell returned, Finn entered the birthing room quietly after the soft knock Trina had trained him in. She'd left a message with his secretary to say they were having a water birth, and even though he'd not long gone he'd been very keen to see the way water and birth 'mixed'.

Trina had given him a scolding glance at his wording, but she had immense faith that once he'd seen the beauty of the way the bath environment welcomed babies into the world he'd be converted. She was glad he could make it.

Sara, the birthing mum, was having her second baby and had come in late in the labour. She'd phoned ahead to ensure the bath had been filled, mentioned she wanted lots of photos of her daughter's birth because she had lots from her son's birth.

They arrived almost ready for second stage and Trina had the bath prepared. At Finn's knock her head lifted and Sara frowned at the sound.

Trina worried. Maybe things had changed. 'Are you still okay if the doctor sits in on your birth, Sara?'

'As long as he stays out of the bath, I'm fine,' Sara said with unexpected humour considering the glare at the door and the contraction that had begun to swell and widen her eyes.

Trina turned to hide her grin and motioned for Finn to enter the room. She liked the way he always waited for permission. Though she might have mentioned it a few times and she had no doubt her eyes betrayed her amusement at his docility. No, not docility—respect. Her amusement faded. As he should.

Finn said a brief thanks to Sara and her husband and settled back into the corner on the porcelain throne, making himself as inconspicuous as a six foot tank could be. Once he was seated Trina tried to forget about him.

She suspected by the way Sara was breathing out deeply and slowly that she'd felt the urge to bear down. Second stage. Time to up the monitoring. When the final louder breath had been released Sara lay back with her eyes closed.

Trina murmured, 'Is baby moving down and through, Sara?'

'Yes.'

'Can I listen to the heartbeat between those outward breaths?'

'Yes.' Bare minimum. She had more important things to concentrate on than answering questions and Trina understood that.

Sara arched her belly up until it broke the surface of the bath water and Trina leaned forward and slid the Doppler low on Sara's belly. The sound of a happy clopping heartbeat filled the room. With her eyes closed, Sara smiled.

After a minute Trina moved the Doppler away and Sara sank back below the water, causing ripples to splash the edge of the bath. She didn't open her eyes when another minute passed and her heavy outward sighs started again.

It took fifteen minutes, and five cycles of breathing, listening, smiling and sinking below the surface of the water and then they could see the baby's head below the surface.

Sara's breathing didn't change, nobody spoke. Below, in the water, the small shoulders appeared. Trina hovered, but Sara reached down, waiting, as an expelled breath larger than the rest released a flurry of movement. The movement heralded the rest of the baby's body had been born. Sara clasped her baby firmly between her hands below the water level and lifted her smoothly to the surface to rest on her belly. The little face rose above the water, blue and gaping, and then the baby's eyes opened and she began to breathe in as the air hit her face.

Everyone else breathed out. The father photographing constantly and the glance the couple shared between clicks made tears sting Trina's eyes. So beautiful.

The birth left Finn sitting thoughtfully at her desk as he replayed the scene.

Finally, he said, 'That was amazing. The mum was so in control, lifting the baby after birth out of the water like that.' He quirked one brow at her. 'How could you stop yourself reaching in to do it for her?'

Trina smiled. 'If she'd hesitated or if she'd needed me to, I would have. But Sara had it covered. That's her second water birth so she knew what she wanted and what would happen.'

He rolled a pen between his fingers thoughtfully. 'I have to admit to scepticism. Why add water to the list of things that could go wrong for a baby at birth?' He tapped the pen on the desk. 'I could see Mum looked super-relaxed—baby just appeared with the breathing, not even pushing, and slowly birthed. Hands off. A very relaxed baby though a little bluer than normal in the first few minutes.'

That was true, Trina thought. 'We find the colour can take a minute or two longer to pink up, mainly because the babies may not cry.'

She shrugged. 'People need to remember no analgesia was needed for Mum because of the thirty-seven-degree heat and relaxation of the bath, so babies aren't affected by drugs for the next twenty-four hours like some are. That helps breastfeeding and bonding. She didn't have an epidural so no drip or urinary catheter either.' And no stitches. Trina always felt relieved when that happened—and it was usually when a mother advanced second stage at her own pace. Something they prided themselves on at Lighthouse Bay—but then they had all the well mums and babies to start with.

It had been a beautiful birth and Trina still glowed from the experience, even after all the tidying up and paperwork had been done.

She glanced at the clock. Finn would go soon. Lunchtime seemed to fly when he came to talk about the births and she could feel their rapport and their friendship, the ease she fell into with their conversations, had all grown this week with his shifts.

Finn stroked the cover of the book Trina had lent him to read on water birth. 'I'm intrigued how you managed to sell the idea here to the board of directors. I know water birth was vetoed at my last hospital.'

It had been easier than expected. One of the board member's daughter had had a water birth at another hospital. But they'd covered their bases. 'Our statistics are meticulous. Ellie has always been firm on keeping good records and it shows we have excellent outcomes on land and water birth. I'm doing the same.' She thought about how smoothly their transition to a midwife-led unit had been in the end. 'Of course it helped with Sam as back-up. Ellie's husband has such high standing in the area now. The local authorities consider us backed by experts even though Sam's not technically here. So water birth with the midwives at Mum's request is the norm here

and proved to be very safe. Just remember we
start with well mums and well babies.'

'Good job. Everyone.' He stood up. Looking down at her with that crooked smile that
seemed to make everything shine so bright
it fuddled her brain. 'Well, you've converted
me. Which is lucky as tonight is my all-night
on-call.'

He gathered up his lunch wrap from the
kiosk meal he'd bought. 'I'd better get back to
the surgery; my afternoon patients will start
to arrive at two. Then my first night without
Piper for a year.'

She knew plenty of mums who would
love to have a night where their babies slept
overnight with someone else. 'How does that
make you feel?'

He shrugged. Apparently not overjoyed.
'Very strange, I have to admit. I think I'm
going to be lonely. Don't suppose you'd like
to join me?'

'If you get forlorn give me a call.' As soon
as she said it Trina began to blush. What on
earth had got into her? Practically throwing
herself at the man at the first opportunity.
But she'd been thinking he'd looked sad when
he'd said it.

She soldiered on. 'What I meant was, unlike Piper, I can go home if you get called out.' That sounded even worse.

His blue eyes sparkled. Mischievously. Suddenly he looked less like an assured paediatrician and more like a little boy offered a treat. 'Now that's an offer I'd like to take you up on. We could get takeaway.'

'Now I feel like I've invited myself.'

He laughed. 'Thank goodness. We could both die of old age before I had the nerve to ask you properly and I've been wanting to since Marni agreed to have Piper overnight.'

He flashed her a smile. 'It's a date. You can't back out now. I'll see you at mine at six p.m.'

She couldn't have him cooking for her after work. 'I finish at five. So why don't you come to my house? I can make us dinner or order in and your mobile will go off anywhere. Do on-call from there.'

'If that's okay, then great. I'll appear at six.' He waved and smiled and…left.

Good grief. He'd been wanting to ask her. Then reason marched in. Wanted what? What could happen if she wasn't careful? It was a small town and she needed her reputation and her just healing, skin-grafted heart needed protection. Was she getting too close to this guy—a guy with a cloud of unresolved questions that even he didn't know the answers to?

Well, yes. She was getting too close.

Did it feel right?

Um, yes. So why couldn't she spend the evening, or the night if that came up, with a man she was very, very attracted to?

Because he was married. His wife was missing, alive or dead, he was still married—and she didn't sleep with married men.

CHAPTER FIFTEEN

Finn

FINN KNOCKED ON Catrina's solid timber door and his heart thumped almost as loudly as his knuckles on the wood. He couldn't believe he was back in the game. Taking risks. Making a play. With his twelve-month-old daughter asleep at a babysitter's and his wife still missing.

He wasn't a villain to do this. He was on-call. Calling on Catrina beat the heck out of sitting at home alone, waiting for his mobile phone to ring for work. And Catrina made his world a more rounded place. A warm and wonderful place.

Different to the walls he normally pulled around himself and Piper. Guilt from the past had become less cloying over the last few weeks, the cloud still there but it had gone from dense and choking to thin and drifting away like ocean mist. Like a new day awakening. Thanks to Catrina.

The door opened and she stood there, with that gorgeous smile of hers that lifted his heart and made him want to reach forward and, quite naturally, kiss her. Which, to the surprise of both of them, he did. As if he'd done it every time she opened the door to him—when in fact it hadn't happened before—and, despite the widening of her eyes in surprise, she kissed him back. *Ah, so good.*

So he moved closer and savoured that her mouth melded soft and tentative against his. Luscious and sweet and…

He stepped right in, pulled the door shut behind him, locking the world away from them, because he needed her in his arms, hidden from prying eyes.

She didn't push him away—far from it, her hands crept up to his neck and encircled him as she leaned into his chest. The kiss deepening into a question from him, an answering need from her that made his heart pound again and he tightened his arms even more around her. Their lips pressed, tongues tangled, hands gripping each other until his head swam with the scent and the taste of her. Time passed but, as in all things, slowly reality returned.

He lifted her briefly off her feet and spun her, suddenly exuberant from all the promise in that kiss, then put her down as their mouths broke apart. Both of them were flushed and laughing. He raised his fingers to draw her hold from his neck and kissed the backs of them. 'Such beautiful hands.' He kissed them again.

In turn, she created some sensible space in the heat between them and turned away.

But not before he saw the glow in her eyes that he had no doubt was reflected in his. They could take their time. The first barrier had passed—they'd kissed, and what a kiss. The first since heartache and they'd both survived. Not just survived—they'd thrived! Finn felt like a drooping plant, desperate for water, and he'd just had the first sip. You could tell a lot from a first kiss, and Catrina had blown his socks off.

Finn slowed to watch her cross the room, mostly because she fascinated him—she walked, brisk and swinging, out through the open door of the veranda overlooking the sea, the backdrop of sapphire blue a perfect foil for her dark hair as distance widened between them.

He tried hard not to look at the bed in the corner of the big room as he passed but his quick glance imprinted cushions and the floral quilt they'd bought on Sunday which she said she'd needed to brighten the place. He pulled his eyes away but he could feel the tightening in his groin he couldn't help and imagined carrying Catrina to that corner.

'Come on,' she called from the little covered porch and he quickened his step. Almost guilty now his body had leapt ahead after one kiss but the cheeky smile she'd flung over her shoulder at him eased that dilemma. She was thinking about the bed too. But not today. He needed to make sure she knew it all. Before he tarnished something beautiful and new with ghosts from the past.

He'd never seen her so bubbly—as if she were glowing from the inside—and he watched her, a little dazed, that he'd done this to her. Lit her up. With a kiss as if she were a sleeping princess. But he was no prince. And it was a long time since he'd lit anyone up like this—just Clancy in the beginning—and look how that ended. He pushed that thought away.

She'd set the table with bright place mats and put out salad and pasta and cheese. Orange juice in a pitcher stood beside glasses and the sunlight bathed it all in golden lights and reflections as the day drew to a jewelled close above the sea.

Like a moth to the light, he closed in on her where she'd paused against the rail overlooking the sea. Her silhouette was willowy yet curved in all the right places, her dark hair, sun-kissed in streaks, blowing in the ocean breeze. He came up behind her and put his hands on the rail each side, capturing her. Leant ever so lightly against her curved back, the length of his body warming against her softness, feeling the give against his thighs.

Then he leant down and kissed the soft pearly skin under her ear and she shivered beneath him; her breath caught as she pushed back, into him. His hands left the rail and encircled her hips from behind, spreading low across her stomach and pelvis. 'You're like a sea sprite up here.' His voice came out low and deeper than normal. 'A siren high on her vantage point overlooking the sea.'

She turned her head and, with a slow wicked smile, tilted her face to look at him. 'Does that make you a pirate?'

He lifted his brows. 'I could be?'

'Not today, me hearty,' she said and pushed him back more firmly with her bottom to suggest he give her space and he let his hands slide down the outer curve of her thighs, savouring the feminine shape of her, and then away.

'Right then,' he said and stepped back. 'Do your hostess thing, sea sprite.'

She spun and pulled out a chair at the table. 'Yes, you should eat in case you get called away. It's Thursday and I know there's a buck's party on tonight before the wedding on Saturday. You might be needed if things get silly.'

She indicated the food in bowls. 'Start now, please. Don't wait for me.' She avoided his eyes and he saw the exuberance had passed. There was no rush and this wasn't just about him—it was about this brave, beautiful widow finding her way to exposing her heart again. He reminded himself he knew how that felt though his circumstances were far different. He wanted to do this right. Right for

Catrina. Right for him. And right for Piper. He needed to remember Piper. And try not to forget he had Clancy in the wings.

Though how could he do this right with a missing wife God knew where and this woman bruised from her own past? He forced a smile to his mouth. 'The pasta looks amazing.'

He saw the relief as he changed the subject and knew he'd been right to give her space.

She gestured vaguely to the hedge that separated her house from the one next door. 'Herbs make the difference. We share a herb garden. Myra does the tending and Ellie and I share the eating.'

She smiled with her mouth but not her eyes and he wondered what she was thinking while she was talking trivia about herb gardens. Had he been too full-on? Yes, he had—they both had—but that had been some kiss. Like a steam train carrying them both along at great speed and only just finding the brakes.

'But it works for us.'

What works for us? Then he realised she was still talking about the herb garden. He had it bad. Just wasn't so sure about her. He stuffed some pasta in his mouth. A taste explosion rioted there and he groaned in delight. And she could cook. His gaze strayed to her.

Time. *It all takes time*, he reassured himself. Took another scrumptious bite and prayed the phone wouldn't ring at least until he finished his food. Preferably not at all.

She poured him some juice, then sat opposite him, her hair falling to hide her face, but something about the hesitant way she tilted her face as if she were weighing her words before she spoke. He swallowed more divine food and slowed down. Then asked, 'Question?'

'I'm wondering if it's too early to ask you about your mother. You said something on Monday that's been driving me a little wild with curiosity.'

His head came up. More because the idea of her being driven a little wild stirred his interest rather than any concern about her prying into his past. 'A little wild, eh?' He speared a pasta curl.

She looked at him and shook her head. 'You're a dark horse, Dr Foley. One bit of encouragement and I can see where that leads you.'

He grinned at her. Spread his fork hand innocently. 'I'm just happy.'

She laughed. 'I'm happy too. So, now that I've made you happy, can I ask you about your mother?'

'Go ahead.'

'What did you mean she was a medium? It's the last thing I expected.'

He'd come to terms with it years ago. Funny how women harped on about it. His sister. And Clancy. Both had hated it. Funny he hadn't thought Catrina would be like that. He'd always thought of his mum's beliefs like a choice. Believe in angels or not. Be a vegetarian or not. Take up ballroom dancing or tarot cards.

'What's to expect? She was a psychologist then became fascinated by the cards and became a medium. I loved her. My sister couldn't have been more horrified if my mother had taken six lovers instead of a sudden attraction to talking to the angels.'

Catrina leaned forward earnestly. 'It doesn't repel me. I'm not sure what fascinates me about it. It's just different. That's all. And a bit out there for a paediatrician to have a medium in his family.'

He'd heard that before. 'That's what my sister said. But it made Mum happy and when she went she went with peace. She died not long after I fell for Clancy.' He shrugged but heard the grief shadowed in his voice. Tried to lighten the tone. 'She said that Clancy had sadness wrapped around her like a cloak and she worried about me.'

Catrina opened her eyes wide.

He sighed. 'I didn't listen.'

CHAPTER SIXTEEN

Trina

TRINA GLANCED OVER the rail to the wide ocean in front of them. Sought the point where the ocean met the sky and sighed too. Of all the things she wanted to ask Finn, she wasn't sure why she'd chosen to ask about his mother. And now that she knew she'd never meet her it made her sad. Another mother gone. It had been a ridiculous question.

Or maybe it was about her because she couldn't remember her own mum, could only remember an ethereal figure tucking her in and singing a lullaby she couldn't remember the words to. But she knew mothers were special. She'd always wanted one and Finn's had sounded magical. Someone who talked to angels.

For Trina there'd been a succession of foster

homes in her childhood, the quiet child, the plain one with her hair pulled back tightly, the one people were briskly kind to but nobody became interested in, except the younger children she seemed to gather around her every time she ended back in the home.

Many kids had it a lot worse, and she'd come to a stage where she'd asked not to be fostered, not to raise her hopes that she'd find a mother to love, and she'd stayed and helped in the home until she could leave. Had worked for a scholarship, always determined to do her nursing.

A nice sensible profession followed by her glimpse into midwifery—and that was when she'd seen it.

The families. Starting from the glory of birth, the connection to the child, the true beginning of a mother's love. The journey she'd make one day because she knew in her bones this was her destiny and then she'd be home. She had so much love to give.

'I'm sorry your mother died. I would have liked to meet her.'

He looked at her thoughtfully and then nodded. 'She would have liked you too.'

The thought warmed her melancholy and she appreciated his kindness. 'Thank you.'

He was the one with the questioning look now. Weighing the difference of needing to know and being too forward. 'Where did you meet your husband?'

So they'd reached that stage. She'd started it. Gingerly she began to unpack it a little. 'Edward was a nurse like me. At uni. We both worked at a restaurant waiting on tables and we laughed a lot. Then we both graduated and went to work at the same Sydney hospital. We married just before I started my transition to midwifery year. He was my knight in shining armour, my soulmate, an orphan like me and a man who understood my need for family.'

She had to admit Finn looked less happy. 'He sounds a great guy.'

She breathed in slowly. To control the tickle of sadness in her throat. 'He was.' Gone now. They'd been so full of plans. 'We were saving up for our family that never came. Because Ed died. Killed by a fast brain tumour that robbed him of speech before we could say much, and his life before we could properly say goodbye.'

She saw the empathy for her sudden loss. Not as sudden as his. But worse.

Finn said, 'That must have been devastating.'

'It was. I sold our flat and came here. Watching the sea helped.' She'd been adrift, swamped by the withdrawal of a future again, the loss of her love and her husband. She'd sworn she would not risk broken dreams again. But then she'd stumbled into Lighthouse Bay and the warmth of her midwifery family had helped her begin the long, slow journey to heal.

'But it seems I'm resilient. Maybe all those foster families in the past made me tough. Because now I'm scuba diving and I've even had lunch and dinner with a man and his daughter. It took two years but I'm becoming braver.' She looked at him. 'But I'm still wary.'

'I understand that.' He grimaced. 'I'm a little wary myself.'

One more question then, Trina thought as Finn put the last of the pasta into his mouth. She waited for him to swallow. 'So how did you meet Clancy?'

CHAPTER SEVENTEEN

Finn

FINN GUESSED HE owed Catrina that. He remembered the day vividly. Puffy white clouds. Brilliant blue sky. Painted ponies and unicorns. 'At a fairground, of all places. She was riding the merry-go-round with a little girl my sister had taken there. A distant relative she'd asked my help to mind for the day. We were introduced by a five-year-old. Clancy knocked me sideways. Her hair—' he shook his head '—just like Piper's, a daffodil cloud around her head.'

He saw Catrina's wince and mentally smacked himself up-side the head. *Idiot. Don't tell one woman another is beautiful.* He moved on quickly. 'I should never have married her. She wasn't that young but she was a child, not a wife.'

'Do you think Clancy knew what she was doing when she ran away? That she planned to stay hidden?'

'I hope so. That has kept me sane. She ran away for a couple of days twice during the pregnancy. I was frantic. Then she reappeared as if she'd never been away and I told myself to stop making a big deal of it. That nobody owns anybody. But to leave straight after the birth?' He shrugged. 'It was a quick labour, but physically it was still a labour. So why would she leave her recovery time and make life hard on herself?'

'What happened?' He heard the gentleness in her voice, the understanding, and, despite his reluctance to talk about a time he wanted to forget, Catrina was a midwife and understood women, plus—he'd kissed her. Planned on doing more. She needed to know.

'Clancy stayed very focused during the birth. Distant, when I look back on it. As if she'd already pulled back from me. Even when Piper was born Clancy pushed her to me and of course I was over the moon. I scooped her up whenever she wanted. Clancy said no to breastfeeding so I gave Piper her first bottle.'

He remembered those first precious moments with his daughter in his arms. 'I've wondered how long she'd known that she was leaving.' He shook his head. Felt Catrina's eyes on him and was glad she didn't interrupt. He just wanted it out. 'So I changed the first nappy, gave Piper her first bath. And when I came back in on the second day to take them home she'd already gone. She'd left Piper with the nurses.'

He saw Catrina's hand cover her mouth but now he was there—in the past—remembered the incomprehension and disbelief. The beginnings of anger and how he'd expected her to walk back in at any moment.

How could Clancy possibly leave her day-old baby? How could she leave him when they were just starting as a family? And the worst. Selfish really. The innuendo that he had been impossible to live with and for what dark reason had she left?

Finn found himself opening his mouth to let those words out too. Ones he'd never shared with anyone else. 'I could feel the side-long glances from the midwives—domestic violence must have run through their minds. Why would a new mother leave her baby?

Was I the sort of man who looked loving on the outside yet was evil on the inside? What had I done to her to make her do this?'

'I don't think so,' Catrina said softly. 'If that were the case, I imagine the mother would take the baby and not leave a child at risk. The staff would have seen how you cared for Piper.' She reached out and laid her fingers on his arm. 'I see how you care for Piper.'

He appreciated that. He really did. But maybe he had done something Clancy couldn't live with. He'd rehashed their short marriage but couldn't see anything. If only he knew why she'd left. 'I don't want the guilt if something happened to her. But I'm well over waiting for her to turn up every morning. My biggest regret, and it still rips out my heart thinking about it—is how am I going to explain to Piper that her mother walked away from her? That's what makes me angry. I can survive but how does a young girl understand her mother doesn't care enough to at least ask how she is going?'

'Every child needs a mother. But Piper has you. I guess Clancy knew you would make

Piper your world. You're a paediatrician so you must love kids. Could keep her safe.'

'Maybe. But to have no contact? Just disappear?'

'You don't know why?'

He shook his head.

'Then you may never know. And it's no wonder you wanted to hide and start again.'

Start again. The words repeated in his head. Yes. He wanted to start again with Catrina. Instead he said, 'Moving here helped with that. Living in our house was pure hell. She wanted the big house, but it wasn't as much fun as she thought it would be. She didn't want a baby, just wanted to enjoy life without worries. She didn't want to be a doctor's wife or a stay-at-home mum. She wanted to be seen with a man on her arm. And I was busy. I guess I did let her down.'

CHAPTER EIGHTEEN

Trina

TRINA LISTENED TO Finn and tried not to judge Piper's mother. Tried not to hear the reverence in his voice when he spoke of her hair. He was right. Of course people would ask why she had left. Would wonder if he'd been the monster to force her into such a desperate act. Would harbour suspicions that somehow he had harmed her. She wondered if Finn knew how lucky he was she'd left the hospital and not when she'd got home, when the innuendos could have been worse. At least he hadn't been the last person to see her.

She tried to comprehend a mental imbalance, or a strange delusion, or just plain selfishness that had made it possible for a woman to leave her day-old baby. To leave without warning, or explanation except for a brief

note, but no assurance of her well-being and
expect her husband not to suffer with doubts
and worry and loss of the family dream all
under a cloud of suspicion. It proved difficult
to imagine. Poor Finn.

'You said you tried to find her. The police?'

'The police agreed the note was real, didn't
find anything and then other cases took pre-
cedence. They didn't have the resources for
runaway wives.'

'You said you hired a detective?'

Finn waved his hand. 'The detective finally
tracked down her last known contact before I
met her, an older man, an uncle, but he'd gone
overseas recently. The trail stopped there.'

Trina couldn't imagine how hard that must
have been. 'She never wrote? Or phoned you?'

'Her phone went straight to message bank
and eventually even message bank discon-
nected. Her credit cards or bank accounts
that I knew she had were never touched. She
didn't drive so they couldn't trace her through
her driver's licence.'

Poor Finn. 'How can someone just disappear?'

'I've asked myself that question many times.'

'Do you think she went with her uncle? Overseas?'

He grimaced. 'It's possible. Or he set her up somewhere. I never met him. Didn't know of his existence until the detective told me.'

'What about your wedding?'

'She wanted the register office. My mother was in her last month and very ill. Half a dozen people came on my side. None on hers.'

It all sounded very sterile and unromantic. Quite horrible really. Not in keeping with this man who adored his daughter and made cupcakes and sandcastles.

She wanted to ask if Finn still loved Clancy. Started to. 'Can I ask…'

Finn's phone rang and they both looked at it vaguely and then reality hit. He was on call.

Finn dug it from his shirt pocket and said, 'I did not plan that.' Then he stood up to listen. Trina tried not to strain her own ears.

Finn left a minute later. 'One of your buck's night boys has cut himself on oysters.' He kissed her cheek. 'Thanks for dinner. And for listening. My turn next time.'

He said *next time*. So she hadn't scared him away. And, despite that harrowing story of his wife's disappearance, he hadn't scared her away either. And he kissed her before he left. Trina hugged herself briefly and began to clear the dishes away. There were lots of reasons not to rush this.

Friday morning Finn met her on her walk and invited her down to his cottage backyard for a barbecue. Despite her need to prepare for the next week of work—washing, sorting, a little shopping—the day dragged until it was time to go over, and her stomach was knotted with excitement when she arrived. This was not being wary.

He looked so good when he opened the door.

He bowed her in. Then he kissed her. Twice. Piper was toddling across the room stark naked and put her arms up to Trina. *Wow.* She scooped her up and hugged her.

'Well, that's a hello anyone would be happy to get.' She met Finn's eyes over the top of Piper's head and her cheeks warmed at the smile Finn sent her. She hoped he didn't think she wanted him naked to greet her at the door. Her face grew warmer.

'Welcome,' Finn said softly. Then changed the subject away from the charged atmosphere of how fast this was all going. 'It's fresh-caught fish tonight. As soon as I bath Piper.'

'Let me.' Trina laughed as the little girl played peek-a-boo around her neck at her father. 'You go ahead. I'll bath her.'

Piper wriggled to be free and Trina put her down. The little girl toddled towards the bathroom. Finn laughed. 'She's getting smarter and faster.' Then he gestured with his hand. 'Her clothes are on my bed.'

So Trina bathed Piper in the little shower tub Finn had made. The enchantment of ceramic tiles with starfish, animals, moon and flowers around the walls of the shower cubicle, a mishmash of words that Piper tried to say when Trina pointed them out.

She loved that Finn had created the novelty for his daughter. Loved the way Piper watched her father with sometimes wise eyes. Loved them both. She sighed.

She was in trouble and she knew it. She'd fallen for him and he was still married. Fallen for the idea of joining their family as pseudo mother and she had no right.

Somewhere there was a woman who did have the right and until that dilemma was sorted she should be spending less time with him, not more—but she couldn't seem to say no. She didn't even want to ask if he still loved Clancy. She didn't want to know.

On Saturday morning she met Piper and Finn at the rock pools on her way back from her scuba lesson. 'What a surprise!'

Finn laughed when she teased him about being predictable and they bickered pleasantly about who was paying for lunch this week after a pleasant half an hour splashing.

After lunch Finn took Piper home for her sleep and Trina went home to make a cheesecake.

She'd been invited to Myra and Reg's for another barbecue; they'd arrived home from their cruise excited about the fun they'd had and eager to talk about the adventure.

Reg was impressed when Trina told him of Finn's assistance during Rhiannon's baby's birth and patted himself on the back for finding such a useful fellow. He rubbed his hands and winked at Myra and then Finn arrived and the story was repeated.

Finn came to stand beside Trina with Piper on his hip. Piper leaned towards Trina so naturally she put her hands out and took her from Finn.

'It's a great unit. I was glad to help.' Finn said as Piper's soft little hands reached up and touched Trina's hair on her cheek. Pulled it experimentally. Absently Trina lifted her fingers to free herself and caught Ellie's raised brows as she adjusted the child on her hip more comfortably. It was clear Piper felt at home with Trina and, judging by Ellie's expression, she was wondering why.

Finn went on, oblivious to the unspoken conversation between the two women. 'Catrina was as calm as a cucumber, as was Faith, of course.' She saw him glance around and was glad he'd mentioned Faith. Faith, Trina and Ellie had been the original three midwives and Faith wasn't there to hear. But it was nice to be mentioned. His gaze settled on Ellie. 'You have great midwives.'

Ellie's questioning gaze finally shifted off Trina, who gave a little sigh of relief. 'I know. Though it's the first time we've actually had to give fluids by a UVC in our unit.'

'Happens a couple of times a year where I worked,' Finn said and took a ginger ale from

Ellie's husband. 'What about you, Sam? Seen many babies need IV fluids at birth?'

'Nope. And don't want to. That's one of the benefits of working at the base hospital. Paeds do all that stuff. Give me a nice straightforward obstetric emergency every time and leave babies for the paeds.'

Finn laughed. 'Each to their own. I'm the opposite. Though Catrina's been letting me sit in on births for the week as a refresher and we even had a water birth.' He smiled at her and she felt her cheeks heat. Ellie winked at her and she tried unsuccessfully not to blush.

Quickly she decided she might as well join the conversation and try to look normal. 'He's converted. It was Sara and you know how calm she is.'

Ellie nodded. 'I was there for her last baby. Gorgeous. I'm hoping to have a water birth,' she told Finn. Then glanced at Sam, who pretended to sigh.

'I'm just the father. But, as an obstetrician, I'd like to go to the base hospital and feel like I have every conceivable back-up plan in place—but I've been outvoted.' He didn't look too worried.

'When's your baby due?' Finn asked Sam

and, seeing the expression on his face, Trina wondered if he was remembering the feeling of being a father and knowing too much—but not wanting to say it.

'Three weeks.' Sam grimaced. 'I'm more nervous than Ellie.'

His wife took his hand and kissed it. 'You're excited, dear, not nervous, and it could take five weeks if I go overdue.'

Sam looked at her, his face softened and he squeezed her hand back. 'I'm very excited.'

Trina decided he was manfully suppressing the *and nervous* addition to that sentence and she remembered that Sam's first wife had miscarried many times. Everyone had their past and their crosses to bear. She should be thankful that she had good friends, wonderful support around her, and now she had Finn. *Be thankful. And stop worrying.*

The night held lots of laughs, tall stories and excitement from Myra and Reg about their cruise. And a few hints that they'd go again soon if Finn was happy to take Reg's on-call roster.

Myra and Trina had shared a bottle of lovely champagne they'd brought back from

Tasmania and Trina glowed with good food, good wine and the joy of having a male dinner partner who fancied her for the first time in two years and didn't mind letting others know.

Finn and Trina left the party at the same time. Trina ignored the arch looks. As they stopped at Trina's gate she pointed to her door. 'You're welcome to come in if you like and have coffee.'

'I'd like that but Piper is drooping and she'll go to sleep soon.'

Trina's previous reservations were muted by the delightful fizz of the pleasant evening and she didn't want the night to end. She could sleep in tomorrow. 'I do have a folding cot in the cupboard. Sometimes Faith's daughter sleeps over if her aunt has to go away. She could sleep in there until you go.'

Finn looked surprised. 'I didn't realise Faith had a daughter.'

'We all have life stories. Her daughter's a real doll. We should introduce her to Piper.'

He looked down at his dozing daughter. Pretended to panic. 'I don't think I'm ready to cope with play dates.'

Trina laughed. 'You're funny.' Then glanced at the door. 'Come in or go?'

'If you have a cot, I'll come in. Thank you.'

Trina led the way, pushed open the door and gestured to her bed in an airy fashion. 'You could change her there and I'll make up the cot.'

Finn nodded and carried his daughter across the room and undid the nappy bag while Trina happily poked around in the cupboard and pulled out the bag with the folding cot in it. She had it out in minutes, grinning a little when it proved difficult to stand upright and kept sagging in the middle.

'I think you're tipsy,' Finn said, laughing. 'Here.' He reached forward with one hand and clicked the last lever into place to make the folding cot stand straight.

'Who, me?' Trina laughed. 'Maybe slightly but this cot is tricky.' She smiled at him a little dreamily. 'It was a lovely night.'

Trina laid the two quilts she'd taken from the bag down on the cot mattress—one as a bottom quilt and one to put over Piper as Finn laid her down in the cot. He put her cuddle bunny beside her head and Piper took it, rolled over and put her thumb in her mouth.

She closed her eyes, secure that she was safe, even though the bed was different.

Trina gazed at the little girl for a moment and then sighed softly as she turned away. 'I'll put the kettle on.'

'Wait.' Finn's voice was low, gentle. His hand on her arm stopped her. 'What was that sigh for?'

'Just because.'

'Because what?'

She sighed again. 'Because you're a great dad. Because you have a beautiful daughter who doesn't seem to give you a moment's bother.' She paused, then finished the thought. 'And I want that too.' Trina felt herself sobering fast when she realised that she'd actually said that out loud.

She pulled away. 'Must be tipsy. Sorry.'

'Don't be sorry. I wish Piper had a loving mummy like you would be. But that's for the future.' Then he turned her and drew her into his arms. 'It was a lovely night. You looked beautiful and happy and I'd really like to just sit and talk and maybe canoodle a bit. What do you think?'

'Define canoodle?'

He stroked her cheek. 'I really, really want to kiss you.'

And she melted. He drew her to the sofa and as he sat he pulled her towards his lap. She wasn't fighting him. In fact she did a bit of climbing on herself. They both laughed. 'So beautiful. So sweet,' he said and then his mouth touched hers and she lost herself in the joy of being cherished.

CHAPTER NINETEEN

Finn

FINN WOKE TO moonbeams spilling across the bed and despite the silver threads of light a feeling of foreboding crept over him. He didn't like it. Splashes of brightness fell on the gently rounded form of a naked Catrina in his arms and he could hear the little snuffles of Piper asleep in the cot they'd moved close to his side of the bed.

They should have waited. His fault. They should have talked about worst-case scenarios if Clancy came back. Should have put in a plan to protect Catrina, but his resistance had been tempted beyond sense once Catrina had climbed onto his lap.

He thought about waking her. Telling her that he would start looking again so he could end his marriage. Protect Catrina from gossip. Gossip that if he stayed would follow her from tomorrow morning when he was seen leaving her croft.

He whispered, 'It might not happen but there's a chance…' But she was asleep. Sound asleep.

Finn slid his arm out gently from beneath Catrina and paused to look down at her in the moonlight. How had he been so lucky to have found this woman—how could he have been so careless to fall in love when he didn't have the right?

He should never have slept with her, should never have let her fall in love with him, with everything still unsettled, and he knew she did love him enough to be vulnerable to hurt, knew she trusted him now, knew he had to fix this if she was ever to forgive him for such carelessness.

He considered waking her then. He'd always intended warning her there was still a chance but the time had never been right to say it again. What they had nurtured between them had seemed so fragile, so new, had happened so fast, he'd feared to destroy it before it began.

Impossible. Fraught with danger. To lose

what they'd just found was unthinkable. He needed to work out tonight how they could move forward with Clancy still out there. But for the moment he could prevent some of the gossip. He'd come back tomorrow.

He wrote a quick note on the back of one of his business cards, then gathered up his sleeping baby, felt her snuggle into his shoulder with complete trust. Like Catrina had. He winced. Slung the nappy bag over his other shoulder and let himself out.

The moon was up, full and bright like daylight, which was lucky as he had no hand free for a torch. Suitable really—he'd been baying at the moon like an idiot, following the siren's lure. Impulsive fool, risking Catrina's happiness.

In minutes he was home, had tucked his daughter into her cot and sat on his own empty bed to stare at his feet.

He should never have slept with Catrina with his wife still out there somewhere.

CHAPTER TWENTY

Trina

SUNLIGHT PEEPED AROUND the curtains in Trina's croft as she stretched her toes luxuriously and remembered Finn's arms. She could almost feel the warmth and strength around her that she'd missed so much and couldn't believe she'd found again. Found again but different. Fairy tales did come true.

It was as if she'd turned into someone other than the broken-hearted woman she'd been for the last two years; she even had a new name. She was Finn's Catrina. Not Ed's Trina. Or maybe both.

She squashed down the piercing guilt and sent love to her departed husband. Yes, she would always love him, but now, after these last few weeks, she knew she loved Finn too. Needed to love Finn. In a different way. But in a real way. Not the ethereal way she loved and always would love Ed. And then there was Piper. Sweet, motherless Piper. She loved Piper too. And, my goodness, she loved life!

How had she been so lucky? She stretched again and wondered what Finn was thinking this morning. She'd found his note.

Spare the gossips—we need to get this sorted.
Finn Xx

Her thoughts took a sensuous turn down the hill towards his house and she was tempted to sneak down there and snuggle into his bed. And him. But apparently, until they told people, they should be discreet. For her sake, he said. But he was the new doctor. For his sake as well. She got that. But what a whirlwind these last two weeks had been.

Maybe a six a.m. break and enter wasn't discreet.

She took her time. Showered in a leisurely fashion. Washed and dried her hair. Applied light make-up though—she stared into the glass with a small curve of her mouth—her well-kissed lips needed no colour this morning. The heat surged into her cheeks. Nor did her face need blusher either. She smiled at herself—a cat-that-ate-the-cream smile—and turned away from the blushing woman in the mirror.

She'd never been that uninhibited with Ed. Their lovemaking had been wonderful but there was something about Finn that drove her a little wild. Or a lot wild. Apparently, she did the same to him. She smiled again.

Her chin lifted. Life was too damned fickle not to take advantage of that fact and she wouldn't be ashamed, and she never, ever wanted to be cold in the night again.

She could grow used to being driven wild in bed. She drew the gaily coloured scarf that Finn had said he liked from the drawer and flung it around her neck. She looked like an excited schoolgirl.

She tried to think of an excuse to turn up that wasn't purely, *Let me into your bed.*

Maybe she could make a breakfast picnic and they could take it down to the beach and eat it on the breakwall? Piper would like that. She could just knock on his door like a neighbour and invite him to join her. Her stomach flipped at the thought of the light in his eyes.

That special smile he seemed to find when she appeared.

She took off the scarf again and made bacon and egg sandwiches, the delicious scent swirling and teasing and making her belly rumble. She was hungry for everything this morning. Even the coffee smelt divine as she made up the Thermos, and extravagantly tucked in a small bottle of orange juice as well. She packed her checked rug and tucked her little picnic bag under her arm as she closed the door.

Then she stopped. Leaned back against the cool wood and sucked in a breath as if someone had thrown a bucket of cold water over her. Finn would be there for her.

For ever? The words trickled through her brain like rivulets of pain on her mind. Questioning. Prodding scarred memories. Undermining her belief in their future.

What if he couldn't? It hit her. What if he wasn't there? What if she fell more and more and more in love with Finn until it was too late? What if something happened to Finn and she'd given the last half of her heart, all that was left of her own self, to him and it got smashed and broken and buried in a coffin like the half she'd given to Ed? What if the worst happened and Finn died and left her for ever? She had said she'd never allow herself to feel that pain again. Piper would go to her aunt and Trina would be alone again. Smashed to smithereens like the broken shells pounded by the surf on the beach below.

She sucked in a burning breath and clutched the ball of pain in her chest. It was too easy to remember the ripping pain of loss. Too devastating to imagine her empty bed now tainted with Finn's imprint so it would always be there. *No!* Nobody could be that unlucky!

She reached out to lay her hand against the wood of the door. Seeking support. Felt the hard wood as a solid force and drew strength from it. Drew another deep breath as if she were one of her mothers and she needed to be coached through a tough contraction. *Okay then.* Breathed again. That wasn't going to happen.

She sagged against the door. Beat it. She'd beaten it. But the voice inside her mind wasn't finished yet.

So, you don't want to imagine that? The voice in her head tried another tack. What if the almost as bad happened and his wife came back and Finn chose her as Piper's mother over Trina? She'd never asked if he still loved Clancy. Had she?

Of course Piper's needs would outweigh hers, maybe even outweigh Finn's, to be fair to him. Either way, she would lose.

Of course Piper needed her mother. If Finn had Clancy he wouldn't need Trina either.

No! They were going to talk about that. Make plans. She straightened her spine. Thought back to the gentle way Finn had cradled her through the night. The whispered promises. The closeness. Finn was a worthy man and she trusted him. And she needed to trust in the future.

Catrina tweaked her scarf reassuringly, lifted her head and a little less jauntily set off down the hill. Felt the promise of the day fill the void. She stopped and closed her eyes and welcomed the sunshine in. Felt it flooding through her body, healing the fear that had gripped her moments before. Opened her eyes and began walking again. A panic attack. She'd had a panic attack. That was what it was. *Silly girl.* Everything would be fine. She clutched the picnic bag and lifted her face again. Smiled.

The sun seemed to be shining with extra brightness today—what was that? Overhead, gulls soared and swooped and she could feel the rocks scatter and pop with exuberance under her every step. The salty breeze brushed her hair across her cheek and it tickled, making her smile. Like Piper had tickled her cheek with her hair. It began to seep back into her. The joy she'd woken with, the excited thrum of blood in her veins. It had been so long since she'd felt this way—excited, alive and happy, yes, happy. Too long. She'd just been frightened for a moment but she was fine now. One night in Finn's arms and she was a goner. But what a night!

Life had certainly taken a turn for the good. New job, new man friend—she shied away from the word *lover* as she glanced down through the trees to where she could see Finn's front door.

There was an unfamiliar car in the driveway and she slowed her steps. Then she remembered Finn telling her about his sister's new car. A red convertible. That was who it would be. *Darn it.* She couldn't be neighbourly when he had a visitor.

Her footsteps slowed. The door opened

and Trina stopped in the lee of a telegraph pole, not wanting to intrude on goodbyes. Three people stepped out. One was Finn with Piper on his hip, clinging like a limpet. Trina smiled fondly.

One was the woman Trina had seen at the restaurant that day that seemed so long ago but was only weeks—Finn's sister. She'd been right. She had a look of Finn.

And the other… Well, the other had a mist of fine flyaway hair the colour of sun-kissed corn, the exact hue of daffodils, just like Piper's. Finn and the woman stood together and only Finn's sister got into the car. Trina felt as if her heart stopped when Finn's sister was the only one who drove away.

Finn and the golden-haired woman turned and went back into the house. The door closed slowly, like the happiness draining from Trina's heart. An icy wind swirled around her shoulders as she stared at the closed door. *Who was that?* But she knew with a cold certainty who it was. Felt the knowledge excising the joy from her day like an assassin's knife. A killing blow. She turned around and climbed the hill like an old woman to her lonely croft.

Once inside she closed the door and locked it. Before she could shut the curtains and climb into bed the phone rang.

It wasn't Finn.

They needed her at work.

CHAPTER TWENTY-ONE

Finn

IN THE MORNING someone knocked on Finn's door. Surely only minutes after he'd fallen asleep just before daybreak. Groggily he sat up, pushed the covers away and automatically glanced at Piper.

Bright inquisitive eyes sparkled at him and she bounced up and down on the balls of her feet, holding onto the top of the cot rail. 'Mum, Mum, Mum,' Piper said gleefully.

'It better not be,' he muttered for the first time but he had to smile. It probably was Catrina. It was good she was here. Though he smiled to himself at her lack of discretion. To think he'd sneaked away to stop the gossips and she'd come at sparrow call anyway. Today he would throw himself on the mercy of the court and find out how to file for divorce. He wanted that new beginning.

Except when he opened the door it wasn't Catrina. It was his sister. Looking shell-shocked and pale. She opened her mouth and closed it again.

'Frances? What's wrong?' Finn reached out to draw her inside but she pulled back. Glanced at her car.

'She's here.'

'Who's here?' He looked at the car. Saw the cloud of floating golden hair and knew. Felt the world slam into him with the weight of a sledgehammer, driving the breath from his body. He leant his hand on the door frame to support himself for a second and then straightened.

Licked his dry lips and managed to say, 'Where did you find her?'

'She found me. Saw your house was for sale in the paper and recognised it. The real estate agent rang me.'

Finn's mind had shut down. He couldn't think. Piper was clinging to him and the door was closing his wife and his daughter inside his house.

One year late.

And—absolute worst—one day late.

Finn shut the front door and turned around to lean against it, the weight of Piper on his hip grounding him like she had done so many times before, and he stared unbelievingly at the woman he'd given up on seeing again.

And, after last night, hadn't wanted to see again. Or not like this.

She was talking. He could see her lips move, though she was looking at the ground as she spoke, so that didn't help the comprehension. Her hair was that floating cloud of daffodil yellow that he'd noticed when they'd first met. Beautiful, he thought clinically, as if he had nothing to do with the scene about to unfold, but too fine; her hair was a golden mist around her head, like Piper's.

She was still talking but his ears were ringing and seemed to echo with the weight of his emotion. She wasn't dead. That was a good thing. That was good for Piper. For the future. Maybe they would have some connection in the future. Not so good for him. He was married. And he'd just slept with another woman. Her timing could not have been worse.

He cut across her long-winded explanations that he hadn't heard a word of. 'Wait. Sit down. I can't understand you when you talk to the floor like that.'

She glanced around a little wildly, her hair a drift of golden cotton in the breeze of her movement, so fine and light it swayed with her like yellow seaweed under the ocean.

He sat down too. Piper stayed stuck to his hip with her head buried into his shoulder. He wished he could bury his head too. 'Why are you here?'

She spoke softly. Hesitantly. 'To talk to you. Talk to Piper.'

He could feel the scowl on his face. Tried to smooth it out. To listen with empathy as if she were a tiresome patient who refused to take necessary advice. But she wasn't. She was his wife who had abandoned them. Remember his oath to treat the ill to the best of his ability. He'd always known she wasn't one hundred per cent well. It didn't help a lot. 'You're a year late.'

'I'm sorry.'

Well, that didn't cut it, but he hadn't heard the reasons yet. He fought the panic that engulfed him. His brain had seized. His chest felt tight. And he had to keep from squeezing Piper too tightly against him. How could she be here? And—the most frightening of all—was he even glad?

He stood again. Turned his back on his wife and moved across to put Piper down in her playpen, but she clung to him. He kissed the top of her head and reached for the fruit sticks he kept in a jar in the fridge.

'Here you go, sweetheart. A bit cold but you don't mind, do you?' Then he put her in the playpen and she sat quietly with her big eyes watching him as she began to chew the fruity sticks.

He heard Clancy's soft voice. 'You're very good with her.'

He stamped down the anger. 'We are family. Plus…' he looked at her steadily '…someone had to be.'

She flushed. 'I made a mistake.'

Really? he thought. *Just one?* But didn't say it. *And it took a year for you to tell us that?* Instead he tried to make his voice neutral and said, 'I don't understand why you would drop out of nowhere like this. What are you hoping to get out of this?'

'Just to talk. At first.'

He winced at 'at first'.

She went on hesitantly. 'See what happens. If what happens is good then maybe—' she drew a long breath and squared her shoulders for a second '—I'm hoping that we could start again.'

Finn sucked in a breath, stunned she could even contemplate that, but then he was in shock. His thought processes were not good. He needed to be calm.

Her shoulders drooped again. 'I could learn to be a mother.' She looked up at him and her eyes were shiny with tears. 'Maybe even a wife.'

CHAPTER TWENTY-TWO

Trina

TRINA PUSHED OPEN the door to Maternity and from down the hallway she could hear quiet moans from the closed doors of the birthing units. Someone sounded very close to having a baby.

In the other birthing room it sounded as if someone else was also very close to having a baby. It happened sometimes. Not often, but when it did at change of shift a third midwife was needed. Technically she didn't start her Sunday call until after eight a.m. but the other midwife had plans for today and Trina was pathetically grateful to be doing something.

She tucked her bag into her locker and washed her hands. The fine tremor of distress was barely noticeable but still she glared at her quivering digits. *Stop it.* She liked and trusted Finn. She would just have to leave it there, parked, until she finished work.

But, deep inside, a crack of loss began to tear and rip and widen. Too soon for loss. She should have stayed safe from pain for a lot longer. Healed more solidly before ripping at the wound.

The woman down the hall moaned louder and Trina drew a deep breath and shut the world outside the doors far away. This was her world. Inside this unit. This was where she needed to concentrate.

The called-in midwife appeared beside her and spoke very quietly. 'I'm in room one with Bonnie. She won't be long. All going well and I have a nurse with me. Jill has Jemma. It's been a long hard labour and slow second stage. Will you take her?'

Catrina was one hundred per cent there. 'Absolutely.'

She turned and knocked gently and pushed open the door.

Jill, the midwife on night shift, looked up with wordless relief. 'Here's Trina, come in to help,' she said to the woman with a brightness that didn't quite ring true. 'You know Jemma and Pierce, don't you, Trina?'

'Yes, I do. Hello there, Jemma.' She nodded to the usually jolly Pierce as well, but his face had strained into taut lines. Some dynamic wasn't working or there was a problem. 'You both look to be doing an amazing job here.'

Then she looked back to Jill as she reached for the handheld Doppler to check the baby's heart rate. 'I always like to say good morning to babies too, so is it okay if I have a listen to yours, please, Jemma?'

'Sure,' Jemma sighed as the last of the contraction ebbed away, and Trina put the dome-shaped Doppler on Jemma's large rounded stomach. Instantly the clop-clop of the foetal heart-rate filled the room. The contraction ended and no slowing of beats indicated the baby had become tired or stressed, and the rate sat jauntily around one-forty. There was even a small acceleration of rate as baby shifted under Trina's pressure, which told her that baby still had reserves of energy, despite what she guessed had been a long labour.

She stared at the large shiny belly and guessed the baby's size to be larger than average. Acknowledged that position for birth would be important to optimise pelvic size.

'He/she sounds great,' she said after a minute of staring at the clock. 'Magnificent belly there, Jemma.' The tension in the room eased another fraction.

'Can I check the position, please?' Jemma nodded and Trina ran her hands quickly over Jemma's abdomen. Confirmed the baby was in a good position and head too far down to palpate. That was good. 'So, catch me up on Jemma's progress, Jill?'

Jill glanced at the couple and smiled wearily. 'It's been a long night and they've been amazing. Jemma's due tomorrow; this is her first baby and her waters broke about four p.m. yesterday. The contractions started pretty much straight away and they came in here about five p.m.'

She glanced at the clock that now pointed to almost seven a.m. 'The contractions have been strong and regular since six p.m. so she's been working all night to get to this point. Her observations have stayed normal, and she's been in the shower and the bath, has tried the gas but didn't like it much. We've walked a fair way and at five she felt the urge to push. I checked and she'd reached that stage already.'

Two hours of pushing and head well down. *Good, not great*, Trina thought. 'Wow, that's a hard and long labour,' she said gently and Pierce nodded worriedly.

'So,' Jill went on, 'Jemma's been pushing for just under two hours now; she's tired and we almost have head on view but it hasn't been easy for the last few pushes. We've been in the bathroom for most of that time, but she wanted to lie down so she's just come back to the bed.'

Trina looked at the night midwife and nodded. In bed on her back was the last place any midwife wanted Jemma if she had a big baby on board. Jill wasn't happy with the progress which, on the surface, seemed timely and acceptable so there must be more.

Jemma moaned as the next wave of contraction began to build and Trina tuned to see why Jill would be worried as the team went to work to support Jemma in the expulsive stage.

Tantalisingly close, the baby's head seemed to be hovering but not advancing that last little bit to birth and Trina kept the smile on her face as she suspected Jill's concern.

Trina moved in with the Doppler again to listen to the baby after each contraction. 'How about you give the doctor a ring and he can be here at the birth? Then he can do his round early and leave early. He'll like that. I'll stay with Jemma and Pierce for this last little bit. You can write up your handover notes here in the room, and that way you'll be ready to go as soon as we have this determined little passenger in his mother's arms.'

Gratefully, Jill nodded and they changed places. When Jill had finished the phone call, she settled herself on the stool in the corner at the side desk and they all rested as they waited for the next contraction.

Trina looked into Jemma's tired face. 'After this next one, I'd like you to think about changing position.'

Jemma sighed and Trina smiled. 'I know.'

Jemma grumbled, 'I just want this over.'

Trina nodded and glanced at Pierce. 'I'm thinking Pierce wants to see this baby snuggled up between you both too. Your baby probably has his father's shoulders, so I'm suggesting turning around and kneeling on the bed or even down on the floor, because that position gives you an extra centimetre of room in your pelvis. That tiny amount can make all the difference at this stage when it feels hard to budge.' She smiled at them both.

'It's a good position for making even more room if we need it after baby's head is born.'

'Is there a problem?' Pierce had straightened and looked down at his wife.

'No. But sometimes when second stage slows this much it means there might be less room than expected. We have set body positions a mum can go into that create extra space in her pelvis. I'd rather have Jemma ready to do that, even if we don't need it, than try to awkwardly scramble into position if we have a more urgent need.'

Pierce nodded. 'What do you think, Jem?'

'I think I'd do anything to get this baby here.'

After the next long contraction a weary Jemma rolled over in the bed onto her knees and rested her head on her forearms on the high pillows that had been behind her. Trina settled the thin top sheet over her and gently rubbed the small of her back. Pierce offered her a sip of water from the straw at Trina's silent prompting.

In the new position baby made progress and the first of the head began to appear on view. There was a soft noise at the door and, instead of old Dr Southwell, it was his son, Sam, and Trina could have kissed him.

Reg was good, but there was nothing like an obstetrician when you needed one. 'This is Dr Southwell, Jemma. Pierce, this is Sam.'

The men shook hands quickly as Trina went on. 'We've some second stage progress since Jill spoke to you, after moving to all fours. There's better descent with the last contraction.'

She moved her hand and placed the ultrasound Doppler awkwardly upwards against Jemma's now hanging belly. It wasn't as clear as before in this position but they could hear the steady clopping from the baby on board.

Sam nodded at the sound. 'Baby sounds good. I'm here as extra hands if position changes are needed.' He went to the sink, washed and put gloves on.

Pierce looked at him. He glanced at his wife and seemed to change his mind about asking more. The next contraction rolled over Jemma and she groaned and strained and very slowly the baby's forehead, eyes and nose birthed. But that was all.

'Keep pushing through,' Trina said with a touch of urgency and Sam nodded. But no further descent of baby occurred. Trina found the foetal heart again with the Doppler and it was marginally slower but still okay.

'We'll try putting your head down. Move the pillows, Trina,' Sam said quietly. Jill appeared at their side and Sam said, 'Phone Finn. Tell him I want him up here to stand by.'

Trina looked up as Jill disappeared and her heart sank. Sam must think it was going to be more difficult than expected.

She removed the pillows and encouraged Jemma to put her head on the bed and stretch her knees up towards her chest with her bottom in the air. It would straighten out her sacrum and, hopefully, give them a tiny bit more room in her pelvis.

The head came down another centimetre and the face cleared the birth canal but then the chin seemed to squeeze back inside like a frightened turtle's head against his shell.

Trina listened to the heart rate again and this time they all heard the difference in rate. Much slower. The cord must be squeezed up between the body and the mother's pelvis. That would dramatically reduce the oxygen the baby was getting.

'It looks like your little one has jammed

his anterior shoulder against your pubic bone, Jemma. Not letting his body come down, even though his head is out. I'm going to have to try to sweep baby's arm out so the shoulder collapses to make room.'

'Do it,' Jemma panted.

'Try not to push as I slide my hand in.' From where she stood, Trina saw Pierce fall back in his chair and put his hand over his face.

Jemma stared at the ceiling and breathed slowly, striving for the calm that was so important, and Trina felt her eyes prickle with admiration for the mother in crisis as she squeezed her shoulder and spoke reassuring words in Jemma's ear.

She watched Sam's eyes narrow as mentally he followed his hand past the baby's head and reached deeply to slide along the upper arm to the elbow. Trina saw the moment he found the baby's elbow and swept it slowly past the baby's chest and face; she saw the relief and determination and wished Ellie was here to see her amazing husband, saw the muscles on Sam's arm contract and watched the slow easing of the limp arm out of the jammed space and suddenly there was movement.

The arm was out, the head shifted. 'Push, Jemma,' Trina urged, and then the baby's flaccid body slid slowly into Sam's hands.

'I'll take him,' a voice said behind Sam and Trina looked up to see Finn there. The relief that swamped her was so great she didn't care that his wife had arrived. Didn't care her heart was broken. No space for that. She wanted this baby with the best paediatric care and she didn't doubt that was Finn.

Sam cut the cord quickly. Trina saw Jill's worried eyes and knew she'd be better at the resus than Jill without sleep.

'Swap, Jill.'

Jill looked up, relief clear on her face. She nodded and hurried over to change places with Trina beside the mother.

CHAPTER TWENTY-THREE

Finn

FINN HEARD CATRINA say, 'Swap, Jill...' as he carried the silent and limp baby to the resuscitation trolley that Jill had set up. The lights and heater were on and Finn rubbed the wet baby firmly. Catrina handed him the next warmed dry towel and he did it again.

She spun the dial on the air and handed the tiny mask to Finn, who started the intermittent positive pressure breaths while she placed the pulse oximeter lead on the lifeless white wrist.

After thirty seconds, the heart rate was still too slow. 'Cardiac massage.' Finn said briefly.

Catrina circled the baby's chest and Finn wondered if this had happened twice in a fortnight before for her. It was unusual. For a low-risk unit this was too much.

He watched as she began compressing the baby's chest by a third in depth. He intoned, 'One, two, three, breathe. One, two, three, breathe.' For another thirty seconds.

Catrina said, very calmly—too calmly, 'Still heart rate below sixty.'

He glanced at her face and saw the fear she held back. 'Thinking about adrenaline after the next thirty seconds,' Finn said quietly, and then Sam appeared.

'I'll take over the cardiac massage, Trina.' He'd be thinking that, as the midwife, she could find their equipment faster.

Trina nodded and Sam slipped in with barely a pause in the rhythm. She reached down and pulled open the drawer, removed the umbilical catheter set he recognised and pulled out the adrenaline. Once you needed adrenaline things didn't look so good.

Good idea about the umbi catheter. He prayed it wouldn't get to that. Finn hoped this baby would breathe before then. Then the big adrenaline ampoule appeared in his vision; the sound of her snapping off the glass top was reassuring. She was slick and he heard her muttering as she began to draw it up. 'The new guidelines say point five of a mil standard; is that what you want, Finn?'

'Yes, thanks. ARC Guidelines.'

He glanced at the clock. 'Next thirty seconds. Heart rate still fifty. Slightly better. Keep going.' He looked at Catrina and nodded at the box.

Thirty seconds later and Catrina had dashed out for the warmed fluid for the umbilical catheter box.

'Seventy.' He saw her sag with relicf. He felt a bit that way himself. *Thank goodness.* No adrenaline needed. No umbi catheter needed. If the heart rate kept going up.

Sam stopped compression and Finn continued on with the breathing. The baby wasn't white any more. Streaks of pinkish blue were coming. The blue on the face stayed but that would be compression of the head causing congestion and that might take hours to go. The body was pink. *Excellent.*

He heard Trina breathe out as the baby's hands flexed, as did his little blue feet. Then the neonate struggled and gasped. And cried. Finn sighed and let the mask lift off his face for a second to see what he did. The baby roared.

He glanced at Trina, saw the tears she was trying to hold back. He didn't blame her. That had been a little too close.

'Good job,' Sam said quietly and Finn looked at him. All in all, it had been an emotional day.

'You too.'

Catrina had gone. Over to the mother to explain her baby was coming over soon. Reassure, like she always did. Being the midwife. To help Jill with settling the woman more comfortably when her baby came across. The baby that was crying vigorously now. Finn felt the muscles in his shoulders release.

Sam said, 'It was in good condition before the cord was occluded by the body. So he had some reserves.'

'They'll have to keep an eye on his blood sugars after that resus.'

'Does he need transfer?'

'See what the glucometer says. Not if his sugars stay good.'

They both knew it wasn't good if a baby had no reserves and got into that kind of bother. Shoulder dystocia was a mongrel. Not common, but fifty per cent of the time there were no risk factors when it happened.

At least this baby had been strong enough to come back with a little help.

Sam had lived up to the glowing praise he'd heard. Catrina had been amazing again. They all were. He could grow to be a part of this team.

Then the real world crashed in. If his wife went away and left him to it. And he still hadn't told Catrina that Clancy had arrived.

He stepped back as Catrina lifted the baby to take across to the mum.

Sam was leaving; he'd go too, as soon as he'd spoken to the parents, explained what had happened, that baby had been fine by five-minute Apgar and he didn't expect any sequelae. Then he'd go, but he cast one glance at Catrina. She was busy. Too busy for his drama. It would have to wait. He just hoped he got to her before she found out.

CHAPTER TWENTY-FOUR

Trina

TRINA SAW FINN leave the room after he'd spoken to the parents. *Good.* She didn't have the head space. He'd come to help when he'd been needed. And gone as well. She'd needed him to go.

She didn't think Finn had known his sister would bring his wife. She wasn't that blindly jealous. She even still had faith that he'd come eventually to explain and thanked him mentally for not attempting that now in the midst of the birthing centre drama. But then again, he didn't know that she had seen his visitor. Guest. Whatever.

Her heart cracked a little more and she forced a smile onto her face. 'Let's get you into the shower, Jemma. Then into bed with your little man for a well-earned rest.'

Jemma had physically fared well. Apart from some grazes, she hadn't needed stitches, her bleeding had been normal not excessive, which could happen after a shoulder dystocia, and her baby had recovered to the stage where he'd fed very calmly, had excellent blood sugar readings and gone to sleep in his father's arms after an hour on his mother's skin.

Finn had explained everything very slowly and calmly and both Jemma and Pierce seemed to have come to an understanding of what had happened. And, without being told, what could have happened. They kept thanking everyone. It was after such a harrowing experience that things replayed in a mother's mind—and a father's. So it was very important the information was given and the chance to ask questions was given.

Trina reassured her again. 'It's one of those things that we practice for. Do drills and prepare for because when it happens we need to have a plan.' *We also had two very experienced doctors available*, Trina thought and thanked her lucky stars they hadn't had a tragedy. For a minute she thought how good it would be to talk to Finn about what had happened, then remembered she couldn't. Maybe never would be able to. Pain sliced through her and she hugged it to herself to stop the heartbreak showing on her face. He'd probably leave now and she'd never see him again.

Four hours later the second birthing mother had gone home with her baby and the morning midwife could take over the care of Jemma and baby. Trina could go home. Not that she wanted to but she wasn't needed here now.

She had time to think. Maybe that was for the best. But damned if she was going to regret the fact she had shown Finn she cared. A lot. And he'd cared about her. There was nothing sleazy in their making love last night. Not a lot of sense either. But mostly the fact they hadn't waited showed a whole lot of bad timing.

It would probably be better if she didn't see him again.

Except that when she got home he was leaning against her front door.

Her heart rate thumped into overdrive and suddenly she felt like crying. She forced the words past the thickness in her throat, looking at a spot beyond his left shoulder. 'I didn't expect to see you here.' Understatement of the year.

'I asked the morning midwife to ring me when you left,' he said. His voice came to her low and strained. 'Clancy turned up.'

'I know.' When she glanced at his face she saw his shock. And, if she wasn't mistaken, his distress that she had found out on her own. The thought brought some comfort. At least he cared about that.

'When did you find out?'

She sighed and shrugged. Pushed past him to open her door. 'I saw your sister drive away. Saw a woman with the same hair as Piper go back inside with you. It wasn't hard.' She felt him come in behind her and didn't know if she wanted that or not. Might as well get the whole embarrassing mistake out in the open. But in private. Her face heated a little and she hoped her hair hid it. She'd let it down when she left the ward, needing the screen of it blowing around her face. Even more now. 'I was bringing breakfast.'

His hand touched her shoulder, the barest skim of his fingers, as if he thought she might shy away from him. 'I'm sorry, Catrina. I wouldn't have had you find out like that.'

What was the optimal way to find out your lover's wife had moved back in? She turned to face him. Saw the sincerity in his face, the pain, and spared a moment to think about just how much his world had been turned upside down by the unexpected return of his wife into his house. If she was Superwoman she'd feel sorry for him. Couldn't quite achieve that yet. 'Where's Piper?'

His face twisted. 'With her mother. Who has no idea what to do with her. Thinks she's a doll to play with.'

And that hurt too. And there was the crux of the matter. Trina had grown up without her mother and, even if Clancy was ditzy, like Finn had given her the impression she was, she was still Piper's real mother. Trina would have given anything to have an imperfect mother over no mother. One who was her very own. There was no way she could go anywhere near taking Piper's mother away from her or Piper away from the woman who'd given birth to her.

She forced the words out. 'I'm glad for Piper. Every little girl needs her mother.'

He sighed. Pulled his fingers through his hair as if he wanted to yank it out. 'Surprisingly, so am I. And yes, a little girl does need her mother. But don't get me wrong. Or get Piper's mother wrong. This is why I need to be here now. Tell you now. Clancy doesn't want to be a full-time mother. She has that "deer in the headlights" look in her eyes. I can see that already and I can't even stay here long in case she runs.'

If he was worried about that, despite the fact she needed to hear this, he should go. 'Should you even be here?'

He sighed. 'I phoned my sister. When the hospital rang earlier. She turned around and came straight back. She's with them at the moment. But I had to come. I need to tell you three things.'

She almost laughed. Tried not to let the bitterness out. The loss that she was only just holding back like the little boy with his finger in the dyke. The whole dam was going to swamp her soon and she didn't think she could hold back the disaster from drowning her for much longer. Her voice cracked. 'Only three?'

He stepped closer. His voice softened.

'They're important. Because you are important to me. Just listen. That's all I ask.'

She nodded mutely. She could listen. Just don't ask her to talk. She was totally unable to articulate the words through her closed throat.

He lifted his chin. Stared into her eyes. And his voice rang very firm. 'One, I'm sorry that you've been hurt by this.'

Yes, she'd been hurt, but she knew it was partly her own fault for falling in love with a man she knew wasn't free. She'd known right from the beginning and still she'd sailed along blithely, ignoring the impending disaster that had come just like she deserved.

He put up a second finger. 'Two. The good part of Clancy being here is that I can ask her for a divorce. Start all the paperwork that was impossible while she was missing. That is a huge thing for us. For you and me. And arranging when and how and the logistics of Clancy's access to Piper so that she and Piper can find the bonds that work for them. To create a relationship that is wonderful for both of them too. Piper will have two mothers.' He smiled like a man with a huge load lifted off his shoulders. 'You and I and Piper can look to the future. But that's where it is. In the future. It will take time and I may have to leave for a while as I sort it all out.'

She nodded dumbly, her head spinning.

He stroked her cheek. 'When it's sorted I will come back and ask you to be my wife properly. Romantically. Like you deserve and like I want too. Like I need to because you deserve everything to be perfect.' He shrugged those wonderful shoulders ruefully. 'Perfection can take a little while, with me. I'm sorry you have to wait for that.'

Trina sagged a little, relief bringing the dam closer to cracking. But the words swirled in her head, glimmers of light beginning to penetrate the weight of the wall hanging over her. He still wanted a future with her. Wanted her to be a part of the big picture. Part of his and Piper's future. Was it too good to be true?

'Three.' He paused. Stepped closer to her and tipped her chin up with his finger ever so gently. Wiped the tears that she hadn't realised were running down her face. 'I love you, Catrina Thomas. Fell in love with you weeks ago. And it's real love. Not the infatuation I had for Clancy. This is I-will-die-for-you love.' He sucked in a deep breath as if preparing for battle. 'We will conquer all the obstacles, my love.' He pulled back to see her face. 'Will you accept my apology and wait, dearest beautiful Catrina, while I sort this mess I made? Please.'

Trina drew her breath in with a shudder, trying not to sob with the relief of it all. The incredible wonder of Finn declaring his love when she'd thought it all lost. The unbelievable reprieve from having to rebuild her shattered heart. She moistened dry lips with her tongue and whispered very, very softly, 'Yes, Finn. I'll wait.'

His strong arms closed around her and she buried her face in his beautiful chest and sobbed while Finn leaned into her hair and whispered over and over again that he loved her so much.

EPILOGUE

A FULL YEAR later in a little pink cottage on the foreshore of Lighthouse Bay, Finlay Foley woke with anticipation and wonder at the change in his life. His two-year-old daughter, Piper, bounced in her cot. She'd thrown out all her toys and demanded to be allowed up to start this most special day.

'Cat. Want Cat. Where's Cat?' She bounced and searched with her eyes. Finn had to smile as he picked her up and swung her through the air.

'Try Mum, Mum, Mum, Mum, baby. You can't call your new mummy by her first name. And your other mummy wants to be called Clancy.'

'Mum, Mum, Mum, Cat,' Piper chanted and turned her head this way and that as if Catrina would appear from behind a chair in the tiny house.

'She's not here. It's bad luck for Daddy to see his bride on the day of their wedding.'

Her little face crumpled. 'Want Cat. Now!'

'I know, baby. Daddy wants her too. I can't wait either. But the girls will be here soon to pick you up and take you to Cat. Then you can put on your pretty dress and watch your daddy become the happiest man in the world.' He hugged the small body to him, feeling her warmth, and wondered again how he had been so blessed to have Piper and Catrina in his world.

The village church at Lighthouse Bay stood with the open arms of two white-columned verandas overlooking the sea. The slender throat of the small bell tower and the skirts of soft and springy green grass that surrounded it had begun to fill with milling guests who had arrived before the groom.

The day shone clear and bright, freshly washed by an early morning shower as if the extra sparkle of purity was a gift from the sky to help celebrate their day.

Finn drank in the serenity, the warmth of those who smiled at him as he crossed the iri-descent grass with his best man, Sam, and the rightness of Catrina's wish to sanctify their union in front of the townspeople and inside the church. He couldn't wait.

The journey of the last few months had taught him to look forward, and that something good—or, in this case, someone amazing—always came out of struggle. He'd learnt to accept that every day held promise, despite the ups and downs, and now his days with Catrina held an ocean of promise that he couldn't wait to venture into.

The minister moved determinedly to greet them as they reached the porch, his kind eyes and outstretched hand reassuring in appreciation of Finn's nerves.

But Finn's nervousness had left—had departed the day Catrina said yes. Eagerness was more the word he was thinking of.

Ten minutes later he was standing at the front of the wooden church in his morning suit, surrounded by smiling townspeople, with row upon row of well-wishers jammed into the little church. All fidgeting and excited and smiling with enthusiasm for the event about to begin. Finn was pretty certain that, despite their enthusiasm, no one was more impatient than he was.

Sam by his side fidgeted too. Probably waiting to see Ellie. He saw Myra, looking particularly stylish in old lace, with Sam and Ellie's one-year-old daughter, Emily, in her arms. He'd been there when Emily was born. Waited outside the birthing room door just in case, to allay Sam's worries, and his own, and been a part of the joy and celebration of their beautiful birth. He couldn't help thinking of that post-birth hour, how such a magic time was one he wanted to share with Catrina when their time came. And Sam would wait outside the door for them. He'd never seen or been a part of such a place that offered so much solid friendship as Lighthouse Bay. And it had all started with the woman who would walk through that door for him any moment now.

The music soared and finally there was movement at the entrance. His eyes strained to see her. Catrina?

Faith, one of the midwives and Catrina's bridesmaid, appeared with his darling Piper in her arms, framed in the doorway. Faith and Piper's deep frangipani pink dresses matched frangipanis in their hair, and Piper was wriggling to be put down. As soon as she was free she toddled swiftly towards him, drawing gasps of delight from the onlookers as she waved a pink sign on a thin stick that read, *Here comes Mummy, Daddy.*

With Faith sedately bringing up the rear, Piper ran full pelt into his legs and he picked her up and hugged her. His throat was tight, his heart thumped, and then Sam's wife Ellie appeared. He heard Sam's appreciative sigh beside him but Finn was waiting, waiting... And then she was there.

Catrina. His Catrina. Shining in the doorway. Resting her hand on Sam's dad's arm, her beautiful coffee-brown eyes looking straight at him with a world of promise and an ocean of love. Finn wanted her beside him now, but he also wanted everyone to see, admire her, as she stood there in her beautiful ivory gown—looking at him with such joy and wonder. Incredibly beautiful. Incredibly his.

Faith reached across and took Piper from him, and everyone turned to savour the sight of the star, Catrina, his beautiful bride, as she stepped firmly towards him with so much happiness in her face he could feel his eyes sting with the emotion of the moment. How had he been so fortunate to win this woman's love? He didn't know if he deserved her but he would hold her and nurture her and protect their love and his darling wife for the rest of his life.

Catrina walked on a cloud towards Finn.

Her husband-to-be. Tall, incredibly debonair and handsome in his formal suit, his ivory necktie crisp against his strong throat. Emotion swelled but she lifted her chin and savoured it. She loved Finn so much, had been blessed, finding him when she had never thought she could possibly feel this way again. The music swelled to draw her forward. She needed no coaxing, couldn't wait, couldn't smile enough, feel enough, be thankful enough as she walked towards the man gazing at her with so much love her feet barely touched the ground.

'Cat, Cat, Dad,' Piper said. Then she looked at her father. Frowned and then chortled. 'Mum, Mum, Mumcat. Mumcat!' she crowed, as if she'd found the perfect word.

The congregation laughed as her parents touched hands and held on.

* * *

Much later, in the cavernous surf club hall, the best party Lighthouse Bay had seen for a year had begun winding down. They'd turned the sand-encrusted, silvered-by-the-sun club-house into a flower-filled bower of fragrant frangipanis and greenery. Tables and chairs and a small dais for the bride and groom all glowed under ropes of hanging lanterns and people milled and laughed and slapped Finn on the back as he stood surrounded by friends. Waiting.

In a screened alcove at the back of the hall the midwives of Lighthouse Bay gathered to help the bride change from her beautiful ivory wedding gown into her travel clothes, a trousseau created by her friends. The laughter and smiles filled Catrina's heart to bursting as she looked around and soaked in the affection and happiness that radiated from her friends. Her family.

There was Ellie, with Emily on her hip, taking back the reins of the maternity ward full-time for only as long as Catrina and Finn were away. Then the two friends would share the duties, two mothers who had been blessed with a career they loved, and a workplace that could still leave plenty of time for family. It suited them both.

Ellie held out the gorgeous floral skirt found by Myra that had once belonged to a French princess. It felt like a caress against her skin as she drew it on.

Myra held the hand-embroidered cream blouse made by Faith's aunt especially for the occasion, and Faith clapped her hands as she began to slide it on.

She had two families now in her full life. In the main hall she had her new handsome and adoring husband, Finn, and her gorgeous Piper, soon to be her adopted daughter, and Finn's sister Frances and her husband, and, of course, Clancy—her unexpected almost sister.

Catrina had grown to care for flighty Clancy, saw that she had not a mean bone in her body, just a little foolishness and a wanderer's heart, underscored by an adventurer's gleam in her eye. Clancy would never be happy for too long in one place. But now, because of Piper and the growing relationship that made Catrina's orphan's heart swell with joy, Clancy could come and share family time with Piper, where she could have the best of both worlds without the responsibility that made her run. With Finn's new family she had people who loved her and people who waved goodbye and let her go.

Catrina noted that Faith, kind Faith, stood alone as she watched them all, watching her daughter chasing after a determined to escape Piper, a whimsical half-smile on her pretty face as she dreamed.

Catrina took a moment to suggest to Finn's mother's angels that Faith should find her own second family and happiness, like she and Ellie had, in the very near future. *Please!*

But then Ellie straightened her collar and she returned to the moment. She was ready and Ellie spun her slowly to ensure she was perfect and the oohs and ahhs of her friends suggested the outfit lived up to expectations. She felt like a princess herself, the beautiful skirt restored to its former glory by Myra, as she floated out from behind the screens to where her husband waited, his eyes lit up.

Finn's eyes found hers, darkened with approval, and she felt a flutter in her stomach at his expression. A look that said she shone like his princess too.

They stepped towards each other and he

took her hand and that frisson of awareness ran all the way to her shoulder with the promise of magic to come. Watching her, his beautiful mouth curved and he raised her hand to his lips and pressed his mouth against her palm.

'I've spent too much time away from you today,' he said quietly as the room swelled with excitement at their impending departure.

'Soon.' She leaned up and kissed him and breathed in the wonderful manly scent of him. She loved him and she couldn't wait until they were alone. 'I wonder how Frances and Clancy will manage with Piper tonight?'

He shrugged. 'One night. They'll be fine. She'll be in her own bed and Marni is on call for them and dropping in tomorrow before we come home, just to check. Then we all go on our honeymoon.'

'We could have taken her.'

'One night isn't too much to ask. I've been talking to Marni. She suggested we should go away every month for one night in the future.' He waggled his brows at her. 'I'm thinking that's a wonderful idea.'

Catrina would take as many nights in her husband's arms as he offered and she had no doubt he felt the same about her. She placed her hand on the crook of his and he captured it there with his other hand.

'Let's go,' he said and, heads high, they walked out into their future.

* * * * *

If you enjoyed this story, check out these other great reads from Fiona McArthur

*A MONTH TO MARRY THE MIDWIFE
MIDWIFE'S CHRISTMAS PROPOSAL
MIDWIFE'S MISTLETOE BABY
CHRISTMAS WITH HER EX*

All available now!